Deepest Obsession

Dark Luxuries 1

Elira Firethorn

To all the people who
fall for fictional men
they'd punch in the face
in real life.

Playlist &
Storyboard

Playlist:

Eyes Off You - PRETTYMUCH

Champagne & Sunshine - PLVTINUM, Tarro

Obsessive - Chase Atlantic

MAKE A MESS - blackbear

Earned It (Fifty Shades of Grey) - The Weeknd

Poison (feat. Krept. & Konan) - Rita Ora

So Damn Into You - Vlad Holiday

You're Mine - Phantogram

Storyboard:

You can find Deepest Obsession's storyboard by going to
pinterest.com/elirafirethorn.

Trigger Warning

Deepest Obsession is a dark romance book intended for people over the age of eighteen. It includes murder, manipulation, mentions of verbal abuse, and sexual assault. It also contains detailed sex scenes that include bondage, semi-public sex (no one sees), edging, orgasm denial, and dubious consent between the main characters. If you think any of those things may affect you negatively, please steer clear of this book. Put your mental health first!

CHAPTER 1

Sophia

Here's the thing about heartbreak—it never goes away.

When I lost my first love at seventeen, I was told the pain would fade.

When I was torn away from everything I knew, I was told I'd eventually be grateful for the fresh start.

And maybe those things are true. But five years after my entire life imploded, the pain still feels just as fresh.

Maybe it's the way the sun is shining today, or how the birds are chirping in the trees outside the coffee shop. They remind me of *him,* and how he once told me that he couldn't wait to see me soar.

Staring out the window, I sigh. Maybe it hurts so much because I still haven't managed to learn how to fly on my own.

I take a sip of my third cup of coffee before grabbing a medium-sized cup and pouring in our house blend. Two creams and three sugars—it's the way Brent always takes his coffee. He comes in every morning before work, usually running a little late.

Glancing at the clock—it says it's 10:04—I chuckle. He's a little later than normal today.

"Soph, can you grab the register?" Lissa, my coworker, asks as she hands some coffees out the drive-thru window.

"Sure thing." I spin around and step up to the counter, only to meet a pair of hard brown eyes that are disturbingly familiar.

As if I needed another reminder of *him.* The universe seems to have it out for me lately.

"What can I get for you?" I say, cringing at the fakeness of my tone. But, unfortunately, it's all I can muster today.

"Sophia." His voice is deep, with a hint of softness. Just the way *he* would speak to me—and only me. "How are you?"

My hand hovers over the register, waiting to punch in his order. But at his words, it drops to my side. That *voice.*

No. It couldn't be. He's too busy running his father's businesses to get his own coffee.

I look up, trapped in the gaze of those brown eyes. And this time, I actually look into them. The same golden flecks that I used to love are still there, along with a darkness that always hovered behind his perfectly-crafted facade of calm.

I let out a breath, taking the rest of him in. His suit fits him perfectly, and his dark hair is a little messy, but in the hot, I-did-this-on-purpose kind of way.

And if he's surprised to see me behind the counter, he doesn't let on.

My stomach sinks. I'd hoped this day would never come—when my old high school friends would find out that I've been working in food service while they attended elite colleges all over the country. But what else would they think? They all witnessed my family's fall from grace.

"What can I get you, Alexander?" I grip the edge of the counter, moving my eyes from his jawline to the screen in front of me. Why does it have to be *him?*

"Medium coffee, please. Black."

I ring it in and tell him his total. As he swipes his card, I watch his hands, remembering the last time they touched me, the last time he held me close.

"It'll be ready in a second." My tone is too light, too high-pitched.

He hasn't taken his eyes off of me. "I didn't realize you were still in town."

Like you actually care.

"Surprise." I give him a weak smile before turning to make his drink.

Just then, the bell above our front door rings and Brent walks in. I can't help but suppress a smile. His shirt is only half tucked in, and his hair is a mess—and *not* in the hot, I-did-this-on-purpose way.

"Here you go." I hand him his coffee at the end of the counter. "On the house."

He gives me a relieved look. "Thanks so much, Sophia."

"Have a good day," I say as he turns and practically runs out of the shop. "And fix your shirt!"

I finish pouring Alexander's coffee and hand it to him, only to find that his jaw is clenched. He's glaring after Brent.

I raise an eyebrow. "Still pointlessly jealous, huh?"

He directs his glare at me. "Excuse me?"

My mouth opens, but words don't come out. Did I actually say that out loud? What the hell is wrong with me?

He steps closer to the counter, gripping his coffee so tightly I'm afraid the lid is going to pop off. "I see you still don't know when it's in your best interest to keep your fucking mouth shut." With that, he turns on his heel and stalks out.

As he leaves, I catch a scent of his cologne—the same one from when we were in high school. Citrus and bergamot. My eyes flutter closed as I remember his lips on mine, his hand pinning mine to the bed, his other under my shirt. How I had absolutely no control but felt the freest I ever had.

That is when I felt like I was soaring.

"You good?" Lissa is giving me a weird look, and I realize I've just been standing at the register, eyes closed, thinking about—

No. No, don't go back there.

I swallow. "Never been better." I glance at the door, but Alexander is already long gone.

It's for the best. It's been almost five years. After I graduated, I was pulled out of his world, *my* world, and I haven't seen any of my old friends since.

For a few more seconds, I let myself remember the way I was his, how he always had a protective hand on me. How I'd melt for him in a matter of seconds. And then I lock the memories in the back of my mind, where they belong.

The past is the past, and that's where it needs to stay.

. . .

For the rest of the week, Alexander comes back to the coffee shop every morning. He doesn't say much to me, just orders his black coffee and glares as I make Brent's ahead of time and have it ready for him.

Brent has been a regular for about a year. His eyes always linger on me, but he's never asked me out. To be honest, he barely even flirts with me—although he does tip well. Lissa says he's just shy, but sometimes I think she's imagining things.

But today, that changes.

"Hey, can I grab a muffin, too?" he says, pulling his card out of his wallet. "A blueberry one, please."

"Of course." I grab a paper bag and the tongs. "No time for breakfast this morning?"

Brent lets out a sigh. "I take care of my mom during the nights. Makes it easy to sleep through my alarm. Feels like single parenting sometimes."

"I'd imagine." I hand him his muffin, then his coffee. "Well, have a great day!"

He smiles, then hesitates. "Did you do something different with your hair today?"

"I did, yeah. Just changed the way I part it." A blush creeps onto my cheeks. It intensifies as I feel Alexander's glare on me. It's like every word that comes out of Brent's mouth makes him angrier and angrier.

"It looks nice." Brent's tone is soft, his eyes kind.

"Thanks." I smile timidly.

Alexander is sitting at a table near the counter, close enough to hear our conversation. I can practically feel the agitation rolling off of him.

I forgot how possessive he can be.

Brent leaves with a smile, and I let out a breath.

Lissa nudges me. "He's got it so bad for you."

"Shut up. I need coffee." My hands are shaking from the caffeine, but at the same time, I feel like I could fall asleep.

It's been months since I've gotten a full night's sleep. Working full time at this place doesn't give me a lot of time or energy, but I don't care. I've gotten myself a new client, and I'm not losing out on what might be the best shot at financial security I have.

"Writing all night again?" Lissa asks.

I nod, watching Alexander perk up in the corner of my eye. He always encouraged me to write. Sometimes, it felt like he was the only one who understood how happy it made me.

"Yeah. I got another client."

"Girlfriend, that's awesome!"

Lissa is possibly the only person in my life who's actually supportive of my writing. Most people think it's ridiculous to try to make it a full-time career.

What am I supposed to do, stay a barista for the rest of my life?

Alexander clears my throat, and my stomach jumps.

"Do you need something?" I say to him, my tone surprisingly even considering his presence over the past week has been turning my insides into knots. I don't know if I'll ever be able to unravel them.

"Sit down with me for a moment."

I glance to Lissa, who shrugs, twirling her pink hair in her fingers. "We're pretty dead right now."

I shoot her a glare before taking the seat across from Alexander. I take a deep breath and instantly regret it. Why does he have to smell so damn good? And why do I have to have so many memories attached to him and his stupid everything?

Staring at the table, I mumble, "What?"

"Come out with me tonight."

Goddamn.

"I don't think that'd be a good idea."

My fingers curl into a fist under the table. High school was a whirlwind romance, but it wasn't meant to last. Not when his father destroyed mine. Not when we were ripped apart from each other. Not when he—

"I disagree. And I know you want to."

My gaze drifts out the window. I can't look into his eyes—the ones that used to be filled with so much passion for me.

"Soph, look at me."

I shut my eyes as he leans forward.

"Tell me you don't want to, and I'll leave it at that. But look me in the eye when you say it."

I grit my teeth and face him. His features are unreadable, but his eyes are as captivating as ever. How can I lie to him? How can I tell him that I don't want anything to do with him when he still haunts my dreams?

"I'll think about it." My voice is uneven.

He reaches into his suit jacket and pulls out a business card. "My personal number. Don't lose it—very few people have it. Text me when you make up your mind."

With that, he leaves, and I'm left as breathless as when he left me the first time. My heart is beating too fast, and I curse under my breath. How can he make me feel this way after all this time? After what he did?

I snatch the business card and shove it into my pocket.

Lissa is giving me a sly grin as I slip behind the counter. "He's cute. You know him, right?"

"He's my ex from high school."

Lissa gasps, her hands flying to her mouth. "And he's still in love with you?! Sophia. That's so sweet!"

Sweet is the last thing it is. But I don't tell her that.

"And I bet he's super rich."

"He is." I bite my lip. *And I used to be, too.*

"Sophia! You have to go out with him!"

"I don't, actually." I shiver, but not from the air conditioning.

"But he's *rich!* And so hot."

"So?" I grip the counter so hard it hurts my hands.

"He's a one-way ticket to financial security, babe. And to you getting to write full time. Is he good in bed?"

Uncannily. "It doesn't matter."

"I bet you're too scared to go."

I shoot her a glare. I know what she's doing, and the playful spark in her eyes confirms it. She may be annoying sometimes, but Lissa loves me, and she's the closest thing I have to a best friend. She's just trying to ignite my competitive side.

And it's working, dammit.

"C'mon, Soph. You haven't been on a date in ages."

"Fine! I'll go."

. . .

I glare at myself in the mirror.

How many more outfits do I need to try on before I find one I'm happy with? Why am I obsessing over this?

Glancing at my phone, I let out a groan. Ten minutes until he comes to pick me up. The thought sends butterflies through my stomach, which makes me resent myself even more.

Why did I say yes to him?

No time to dwell on that now. I slip on a sleeveless pink dress that hugs me in all the right places and falls to the middle of my thighs. It's sexy as hell. Maybe too sexy. But this way he's seeing what he missed out on.

I bite my lip, pulling my hair up into a simple yet elegant bun. *That's all this is. You're not dressing up for him.*

There's a knock on the door downstairs, and I freeze, but then let out a small laugh. Of course he's early—he always was.

Grabbing my most comfortable pair of heels, I rush downstairs and swing the door open—just for my heart to stop.

He's changed out of the suit he was wearing this morning at the shop, but he's still wearing a button-up and pants that I have to tear my eyes away from. God, he even rolled up his sleeves.

Gulping, I step back to let him in. "I'm almost ready."

His eyes take me in, drifting up and down my body. "You look perfect."

As he passes me, his cologne drifts my way, and I dig my nails into my palms. It brings back so many memories, so many feelings.

"Listen, I want this to be a one-time thing," I blurt out. "Catching up is fine, but I don't want to date you."

"Of course, little bird."

I freeze as my stomach flips. Did I hear him correctly? "Don't play games with me," I hiss.

He looks me up and down again, his eyes burning with something—lust? Anger? Passion? I'm not quite sure. "Go finish getting ready, Sophia."

I grit my teeth. I was about to, but now that I've been told to, I just want to slap him across his stupidly perfect face. Instead, I turn on my heel and head back up to my room. I grab my phone and my ID, and then check myself in the mirror.

I really do look perfect.

Turning, I make sure the small tattoo of a bird in flight is hidden by the back of my dress. *Little bird.*

I can almost feel his hands gripping my hair as he gave me a gentle kiss on the tip of my nose, calling me his.

A shiver traces up my spine, and I shake myself out of my trance. I can't let my mind go back there. I can't lose myself in him again, no matter how tempting it is.

I head back downstairs, gripping the railing as I feel his gaze on me. "Ready?" I don't meet his eyes.

He opens the door, and I step out, jumping when I feel his hand on my back. It's firm, but warm, and it sends sparks through my body.

The porch steps creak as we make our way to the sidewalk, almost a reminder that we're now separated by two very different worlds. Alexander probably hasn't stepped inside a house this rundown in his entire life. And I haven't seen the inside of a mansion since my senior year of high school, thanks to his father.

It isn't his fault.

Forcing a smile as he opens the car door for me, I slide onto the leather seat. I expect him to shut the door, but he doesn't. He has one hand on the door, the other on the roof, and he's staring at me with a dark hunger in his eyes.

"The view better than you remember?" *Shit, shit, shit. Why would I say that?*

His eyes flit to my legs before meeting mine again. "Much." With a smirk, he slams the door and gets in on the other side, then nods at the driver in the rearview mirror.

We're out of my neighborhood in a few minutes, and from the looks of things, we're headed downtown. Old houses with unmowed lawns have turned into rows of storefronts. We pass by the coffee shop I work at.

"Where are we going?" I give him a small glance. He's staring at me. That look of hunger hasn't left his eyes.

"You'll see."

Sure, I have some idea of what he has planned. It's already late, and most places are closed. Even so, I'm a little nervous about being out with a practical stranger in the middle of the night.

For the rest of the drive, we ride in silence. I scroll through a few apps on my phone to distract myself from the jitters of having Alexander this close to me again, but it doesn't work. My heart is going crazy. My palms are sweaty. And my mind is tempted to wander to places it shouldn't go.

But then the driver slows to a stop, pulling over, and Alexander gets out. I hesitate, wondering if I could ask the driver to get me out of here so I don't have to spend the night with this man.

But then my door opens, and I'm taking the hand that's reaching out to me, letting Alexander pull me up and into his arms.

Fuck.

He holds me close for a second. I know I couldn't get away even if I wanted to. But he releases me and returns his hand to my back, guiding me up the sidewalk and past a long line.

As we approach the front of the line, a bouncer in all black nods at Alexander, stepping aside and letting us pass.

Inside, I'm hit with flashing lights and pounding music. Alexander pulls me onto the dance floor, his hands on my hips, and I can't help but sway to the music.

I let out a laugh, raising my hands in the air and watching Alexander watch me. For a moment, we're at prom, head-over-heels for each other, a little tipsy from the alcohol he stole from his father.

Before I can stop myself, I let myself fall into him. "We should get drinks," I yell over the music. God, his eyes are perfect.

For a second, he stares at me, and I wonder if he didn't hear me. It's like he's looking straight into my mind, into my memories, and seeing how much I cherish the last time we were like this.

But then he pulls away and nods. "Stay here."

The second he's gone, a sense of vulnerability washes over me. I've never gone clubbing alone before, and I've always made sure I had a friend by my side.

You'll be fine, Sophia.

With a glance behind me, I keep dancing. It's been too long since I let loose. My roommates ask me out with them all the time, but I usually make some excuse. I keep telling myself that soon I'll be able to write full time and quit my job, and then I'll have time for fun.

But now that I'm here, I'm beginning to think that I have the wrong idea.

A hand on my hip makes me turn. Alexander got those drinks fast.

But I find a pair of sharp green eyes staring back at me, instead of Alexander's soft brown ones.

"T-Tristan?" I stumble backward, only to bump into someone. He's barely changed a bit. Light ruffled hair, terrifying eyes, and sharp cheekbones.

"I never thought I'd see you here." He steps closer to me, and when I try to squirm away, he holds me close to him. "You're more the stay-in-and-read type."

My chest tightens. I dated Tristan for a few months before Alexander, and it was a rollercoaster of manipulation, anger, and bullying. Needless to say, Tristan Goodwin is the last person on this planet I'd like to run into.

"Fuck off." I shove him away, but he doesn't budge.

"Just dance with me." His fingers are digging into my hips, and there's a sadistic twinkle in his eyes.

Looking around at all the bodies crammed onto the floor, I contemplate screaming. But is making a scene worth it? He just wants a dance. And Alexander will be back soon.

"I've missed you," he says into my ear, and I shiver.

"Can't say the same."

While Alexander was a catalyst to finding the little bit of freedom I had in high school, Tristan kept me in a mental cage. He could get under my skin with a few words and force me to do anything for him with a few more.

Fuck this.

I turn around, letting him grind against my ass. Then I slam my heel onto his foot as hard as I can manage. But he just grips my hips tighter, pulling me close until my back is against his chest.

"Careful, Sophia, or I'll have to punish you. But you'd like that, wouldn't you?"

"You're disgusting." I elbow him in the ribs, but he just laughs.

Everyone around us is too drunk and self-absorbed to notice my struggle, and the music is too loud to hear us arguing. But I continue trying to squirm out of his grasp.

He leans down and bites my earlobe. "Just dance with me or I'll drag you out of here before you even have a chance to scream."

I still, my breath frozen in my lungs. He whirls me around so I can see his satisfied smile.

"Much better. Now dance."

"You mons-"

"Get your fucking hands off of her, Goodwin."

I snap my head around to see Alexander glaring at us. No, not at me. At Tristan. Relief floods my body.

Tristan releases me, shoving me toward Alexander. "Of course she's with you. You never quite got over her, did you?" His eyes cut to me. "Piece of trash."

Then he disappears into the crowd.

Without a glance, Alexander hands me my drink and pulls me to the side of the room. It's packed in here, but people seem to move out of his way the second he looks at them.

"I'm fine," I shout, but the truth is I'm shaking so badly I've spilled the blue liquid in my cup all over my hand.

"Just sit."

The leather couch against the wall is mostly full, but there's a spare seat on one. He slides onto the edge and then pulls me onto his lap. As he does, I lose my balance and start to fall—but he keeps me upright, his free arm wrapping around me.

My lips part as I realize how close I am to him. I can smell the alcohol on his breath and feel the intensity of the way he's looking at me.

"Do you want some water?"

"Wha-no, this is fine." I sip the liquid in my cup. It's sweet, but I can still taste the alcohol. Smiling, I look up at him. He remembered that I don't like straight alcohol. I don't care how old I am, I just can't drink it alone.

For now, I let myself relax. The feeling of security is back now that I'm with Alexander and Tristan is nowhere to be seen.

What are the odds of running into him here, while I'm out with Alexander? It almost seems too unrealistic to be a coincidence.

I suppress a shiver as I think back to his hands gripping my hips. How I couldn't get away from him. How he threatened me. What would've happened if he'd decided that he wanted more than a dance?

Don't think about it, Sophia.

I need a distraction.

Quickly, I down the rest of my drink and stand. "Let's dance."

Without hesitation, Alexander leads me to the dance floor. We dance, and as the alcohol hits me, I let myself go. The blur of the lights and the vibrations of the music in my chest are euphoric.

Before I know it, we're three drinks in, my hands have stopped shaking, and my encounter with Tristan is a distant memory.

Alexander hasn't left my side the entire night. In fact, he's barely taken his eyes off of me.

And I wouldn't have it any other way.

As the lights flash above us, I press my body to his and wrap my arms around his neck. Our lips are mere inches apart, and I feel his body tense.

"Sophia." It's a warning, the gift of an option to back off and change my mind—which he doesn't give often.

But I just smile at him and sway my hips, letting my lips come even closer to his. Who was I to think I could stay away from him? His scent is intoxicating, a mix of sweat and citrus and *him*.

He may look older, but on the inside, he's still the same boy who kept me safe from the bullies at school.

Still the same boy who snuck into my room in the middle of the night on my seventeenth birthday.

Still the same boy who kissed me like I was the only thing keeping him alive.

"Come with me." His voice is gruff, like he's restraining himself. He pulls me into a dark corner and presses me against the wall.

My body is full of butterflies as he leans down until our lips are almost touching. For a moment, he hesitates, his eyes flitting up to meet mine. They're dark, filled with lust.

His arm tightens around my waist, eliminating any space between us, and then his mouth descends onto mine. A small moan escapes my mouth, probably lost to the sounds of the club, as he kisses me.

My eyes flutter closed, and I relax into him, wrapping a hand around the back of my neck. He's kissing me with such passion, such hunger, it's almost like not touching me for the last five years almost killed him.

When he finally pulls away, I'm gripping the collar of his shirt. I'm eighteen again, surrendering myself to him, letting his hands travel farther up my thighs . . .

Alexander groans, his lips brushing mine again. "I need to get you out of here."

My heart leaps. For a moment, I almost get ahold of myself and tell him no. But then I just smile up at him and nod.

Maybe it's the alcohol. Maybe it's how good he feels. Or maybe it's how much I've missed the freedom only he's able to give me.

He kisses me again, and I see pain on his face when he pulls away. Then he's guiding me through the crowd, back outside, and into the back of his car.

We take off without more than a nod to the driver, and Alexander pulls me into his lap, his hands cupping my ass. He kisses my jawbone, my neck, my collarbones.

"Alexander," I whisper. "We're not alone."

He slips the strap of my dress off my shoulder. "He doesn't care. This is what he's paid to do."

Jealousy tinges my thoughts. Does he do this often with other women? But before I can ask, Alexander brushes his thumbnail over my nipple through the thin fabric of my dress.

My back arches at his touch.

Then he grabs me and turns me so my back is pressed against his chest, my head resting on his shoulder. His hand is on my dress, trying to pull it down to uncover my breast, but the fabric won't give. Until he yanks the strap, ripping it off, and jerks my dress down.

Gasping, I glance at the driver. The layer of plexiglass gives us a tiny bit of privacy, but if he were to glance at his rearview mirror—

Two fingers pinch my nipple, hard, and I squirm at the pain.

Without a moment's hesitation, Alexander forces my thighs open and pulls my thong to the side, exploring me.

His fingers feel like fireworks. I moan as he works my clit and my nipple, more gently this time.

He holds me there, kissing my jawline, undoing me with just a few fingers.

I shudder, struggling to keep my eyes open. Bliss—this is bliss. No one has ever been able to do me the way he has, and now that he's here, touching me, exploring me . . . How could I ever let this go?

The car slows to a stop, and I grip his leg, my eyes opening. It's just a stoplight. The driver's eyes are still on the road. For now.

"That's right, little bird," Alexander whispers in my ear. "All it'd take is a glance—either from him or anyone driving past us. They'd see you splayed out on my lap, exposed and shaking and needing more."

He pinches my nipple, and my eyes roll into the back of my head. My lips part, but no sound comes out.

"Did you think I'd forget that you're a naughty little exhibitionist, Sophia?"

A whimper escapes my mouth, and then the first wave hits me. My body jerks, and his hand moves to cover my mouth and stifle my cry. His arms hold me still, entrapping me while setting me free, as he continues with feather-light strokes on my clit until I'm quivering in his arms.

"That's it, little bird." He kisses the side of my head. "Now get on your hands and knees."

I instantly obey, crawling off of him and kneeling on the seat. He's unzipping his pants, and I watch with a hunger I've tried to suppress for years. When his cock pops out of his underwear, I let out a tortured whimper.

"Lick."

For a moment, I don't move, just taking him in as streetlights wash him in golden and red hues. His dark hair is messy now, falling over his forehead. The top buttons of his shirt are undone. He looks like a god.

"*Now.*" Alexander grabs my hair and shoves my face down.

I take his tip into my mouth and moan. I've thought about this more times than I care to admit—the way he felt in my mouth, how much I loved the way he grabbed my hair and moved me around.

I lick his shaft up and down, gripping his legs as he shudders. He grinds against my lips, and I open, just for him to thrust himself into my mouth.

"Fuck, Sophia." He holds my head in place, hitting the back of my throat over and over again.

I gag a bit—it's been a while since I've done this—but don't pull away. Not that I could. *Not that I want to.*

After a minute, he slows, panting. His grip on my hair loosens, and I move my head up and down, stroking him with my tongue as I do. Then I reach one of my hands down to cup his balls and suck on his tip, circling it with my tongue.

He moans, and I feel his hand tightening around my hair again. "Still can't get enough of my cock, can you?"

In response, I take as much of him in as I can. And then he takes control again, shoving my head up and down. I let out a strangled groan, but he only goes harder.

Tears drip from my eyes, falling onto his legs. I give his balls a light squeeze, and he grunts as his cum coats the back of my throat in spurts.

I swallow it all, and when he releases my head from his grasp, I cough and choke in air. A tear falls onto my cheek, and he brushes it off with his thumb.

"Now clean up the mess you've made."

I lower myself back down to his cock and lick it clean, sucking the last bit of cum out of him. His hand rests on my back. Not in a controlling way. More a reminder that just mere minutes ago, he had me quivering and coming, and he can do it again whenever he pleases.

I settle into the middle seat, as close to him as possible, as he tucks himself in. Then he pulls my seatbelt over me and clicks it in, giving me a small kiss on my hairline.

"Where are we going?" I ask, readjusting my dress to cover myself up again—which doesn't work too well, considering Alexander tore the strap off the one side.

"My home. I want to see you in it."

Biting my lip, I run my fingers up and down the seatbelt. I was at his parents' house all the time when we were in high school. I hadn't thought that he would've moved out, even though it makes sense. Especially after his father died.

I wouldn't want to live in a house that constantly reminded me of a dead person, either.

In a few minutes, we pull up to a dark mansion, and I gasp. It's *huge*.

Of course, I don't know what else I expected. Alexander's father owned a group of big tech companies, and from what I heard, Alexander inherited everything.

We slow as a gate opens, pulling into the driveway and up around a gurgling fountain.

"Alexander, this is beautiful," I whisper, peering out the window at the three-story mansion.

He watches me silently as we pull into the garage. When my eyes meet his, I expect him to look away, but he doesn't. But then the driver opens my door, offering his hand to help me out.

I thank him, stumbling a bit as I step onto the concrete. Half my attention is diverted toward not letting my dress slip down my boob. Which may not matter, since he probably heard us—and possibly saw me. After a certain point, I was lost to the fact that there was another person in the car with us.

Alexander places a hand on my back and leads me down a hallway, and then up a small set of stairs. A light flicks on automatically, revealing an expansive room with vast windows looking over the yard and the trees in the distance. A hot tub bubbles in front of the windows.

I let out a breath, taking in the view. "Did you design this?"

Alexander loved designing houses and buildings in his spare time. Architecture always fascinated him, and I always gave him plenty of ideas. We used to dream up lots of different houses that we'd live in one day.

"Maybe. Now, join me."

I turn to find him stripping out of his clothes. He nods to a white bikini sitting on one of the chairs.

"Alexander—"

"Unless you'd prefer to join me naked." He stands in front of me, posture straight and confident. I didn't think it was possible for him to look hotter than he did earlier, but with all his clothes off, I can barely stop staring at his muscles, his abs, that delicious V leading down to—

God, he's hard again.

"I . . ." My breaths are coming short and quick. I can't tear my eyes away from him.

He steps toward me, taking my wrist and pulling me into him. His breath tickles my neck. "Don't make me make you." He kisses the sensitive skin below my ear.

I gulp, ignoring the throbbing between my legs. "Xan . . . Alex . . . Alexander—" I freeze when I feel his hands on my back, unzipping my dress and letting it fall to the floor. He pulls down my thong, kissing my stomach as he does.

"Step."

I grab onto his shoulders, stepping out of my thong. He straightens and moves back. A smirk forms on his lips as he takes me in, completely naked except for my heels.

"Much better. Now, what do you prefer? Naked, or the bikini?"

I open my mouth, but no words come out. Did he plan this? Has he been waiting to undress me all night? All day? Ever since he asked me out?

"Answer or I'll decide for you, little bird."

"Bikini," I force out.

He picks up the bottom piece and kneels down, holding it open. "Come on."

I step into it, and he pulls it up, his lips dragging up my right thigh as he does.

Fuck. I don't know if I can handle him tearing me apart again tonight.

He grabs the bikini top. It's just a couple of triangles with strings holding it together. He slips it through my arms, positioning it over my breasts before tying it together in the front.

No doubt he chose this one on purpose, too. Easy to take it off whenever he wants.

With a hand on my back, he leads me to the hot tub. He steps in first, making his way down the stairs. I watch as the water envelops him and steam curls around his muscled body. He turns when he's waist-deep, looking me up and down.

"I suppose you should take your heels off. Regrettable."

I snap out of my trance and kick them off, then walk to the edge of the water, forgetting about the stairs. After lowering myself so I'm sitting on the ledge, I dip my legs in. It's always taken me longer to get used to the high temperature of hot tubs.

Taking a seat and leaning back, Alexander watches me closely. There's a hunger in his eyes, but there's something else, too. A darkness—the same kind that showed up when he confronted Tristan at the club.

It's a part of him that I let fade from my memories over the years. It always scared me, but it comforted me, too. When we were together, I knew he'd do anything to protect me.

Except stop his father from ruining yours.

Gripping the ledge of the hot tub, I try to shake off the feeling. We were teenagers. What could he have done?

Warned me. Taken me away from it all.

"Are you all right?" Alexander's voice is deep and low, laced with concern.

I realize there are tears in my eyes. Blinking them away, I slide into the tub, ignoring the heat as it bites at my skin. "Just remembering."

He pulls me onto his lap effortlessly, locking me in. I place a hand on his arm, and his muscles tense. "Tell me more."

My lips part slightly, but then I shake my head. There's no way we're talking about our parents. "What was your favorite part of us?"

It's a question I shouldn't be asking. I told him this was a one-time thing, and I meant it. I still do. But I've always wondered if he still thinks about me. If he regrets me. Or if he misses me.

"You." He brushes a stray hair behind my ear. "All of you. Your laugh, your gentle voice, the way you clung to me when you fell asleep in my arms. How you could never get enough of me."

An ache blooms in my chest, and I can't look him in the eyes. "I always felt safe with you." *And free.*

We sit in silence for a moment, his hand running up and down my spine. I let myself pretend that we're eighteen, that our parents didn't have the mysterious falling out they had. That our futures are still hopeful and intertwined with each other's.

But then Alexander breaks the silence. "Why are you here?"

I don't answer, and he places two fingers under my chin and lifts, forcing me to look at him. His face is mostly unreadable, but there's a hint of curiosity in his eyes.

But I haven't been able to figure out why I said yes.

Is it because I just wanted a break from the mundane reality of my life? Because I miss the luxury of living in a mansion and not having to worry about money? Is it because I know that if I play my cards right, Alexander is a one-way ticket to financial security?

As I bring up a hand to trace his jawline, I can't help but feel that there's more to why I came out with him tonight. That a part of my heart—if not the whole thing—will always ache for Alexander. Will always *belong* to him. And I can't deny the fact that I've never quite gotten over him.

But none of that changes the fact that five years ago, he ripped my heart out of my chest and left me bleeding out. And then his father somehow managed to dissolve my father's companies and reputation until there was nothing left except a pile of ashes.

"Sophia."

I don't know what to tell him. So I slip a hand behind his neck, nestling closer in his lap, and press my lips to his. At first, he stays stiff, unsure if he can trust this. But then he deepens the kiss, caressing my neck.

And then I'm shifting so I'm straddling him, and his hands are gripping my ass. My hands explore his chest, more muscled than it was when we were kids.

"I loved this, too," Alexander says in between kisses. "I miss the way we craved each other. I miss ripping all of your clothes off and claiming you as mine. I miss the way I could have you wet whenever I wanted, even if we were fighting."

My back arches as his fingers trace the fabric of my bikini until they reach in between my legs. Little shots of electricity zap from his fingers, and I let out an involuntary moan.

"I miss you begging for me," he whispers lowly in my ear.

I melt into him, panting for breath and realizing my fingers are gripping his shoulders like he's my lifeline.

"I miss the way you felt, the way your little cunt would clench right before you'd come. I miss your taste, your moans, your screams." With his free hand, he grips the back of my hair and pulls my head back, exposing my neck. "I miss the way your skin felt in my mouth."

He buries his face into my neck, kissing and sucking. Without my permission, I find my hips grinding against him, making him groan. A bite on my skin makes me gasp, but he instantly soothes the pain with a kiss.

"Xander," I moan. "I need you to . . ." I trail off as his lips move down to the tingling skin in between my breasts.

"Yes?" He releases my hair and pushes the fabric of my bikini to the sides, revealing my breasts.

"I need you to—*fuck*, Xander." My head falls back.

He's sucking my right nipple, letting his tongue run over it, causing a shudder to run through my body. He releases me to say, "Spit it out, little bird."

"Fuck me," I whisper.

"What was that?" He licks my left nipple so lightly I almost scream.

"I need you to fuck me, Xander."

"Is that so?" He runs a finger down my spine.

"Please." My voice shakes as I grind against him. He's so, so hard. I move to undo the bikini, but he grabs my hands.

"I don't think so. You wanted to wear the bikini. Now you'll deal with the consequences." He lifts me up and practically throws me onto the floor above us. The tiles are cold and hard on my back, but I don't care.

Alexander stays in the water, yanking my thighs apart and shoving the bikini bottoms to one side. Without a moment's hesitation, he buries his face in between my legs, and I have to stifle a scream.

His tongue circles my clit, and he groans. Then he licks me slowly, up and down, before pulling away and leaving me throbbing. "You taste just as good as I remember."

I prop myself up on my elbows and watch him as he dives back in, thrusting his tongue inside of me. I squirm, but he holds my hips in place as he pulls out and caresses my clit with his mouth.

"Fuck," I whisper, closing my eyes to the mini explosions he's setting off inside my body.

As I let out a moan, he sucks my clit, thrusting two fingers inside of me. He presses against my walls, the tip of his tongue flicking my clit, and an unintelligible sound escapes my mouth. He does it again and again, increasing pressure, as pleasure builds up inside of me.

"Xander, I'm going to—" I let out a cry, squirming and writhing under his mouth. My legs kick, splashing water everywhere. But he holds my hips in place, lightening the pressure on my clit but still licking away. My eyes roll back into my head as my body jerks one last time.

Finally, he pulls away, peppering my inner thighs with kisses. Then he hauls himself out of the water and turns me so I'm parallel to the ledge, my legs no longer in the water. In a second, he's on top of me, pushing my legs open. His mouth crashes into mine, and I wrap my arms around his neck.

But he breaks away from me, and I feel something warm and hard sliding toward my entrance. His gaze meets mine, and then he thrusts into me with all his strength. Something between a whimper and a scream leaves my lips as he grabs onto my shoulders to keep me from sliding away from him. Then he pulls out, just to slam inside of me.

"Fuck, Soph," he says as I clench around him. He slows down, pushing himself up a bit and snaking a hand downward.

I whimper as my overly-sensitive clit jumps back to life at his touch. But he pushes through my squirms as his cock finds one of my sensitive spots, hitting it over and over again.

At some point, my eyes slide closed and I lose control of the sounds coming out of my mouth. Alexander pushes me closer and closer to the edge.

He groans, and I reach up to grab his arm. I'd never forget that sound. He's close. My eyes open, and I find him watching me. Then he slams into me, picking up the pace, not letting up on my clit.

He lets out another moan, and the sound of it pushes me over the edge. I cry out, my back arching, my nails digging into the skin of his arms. Finally, he eases his finger off my clit as he releases into me, his eyes closed.

Then he collapses onto me, still throbbing inside of me, and whispers in my ear, "You feel even better than I remember."

I let out an uneven breath, resting my shaking hands on his back. "So do you."

We lay there for what feels like hours but is probably just a few minutes. As we come back down to earth, he kisses my neck lightly and climbs off of me. There are a couple of towels on one of the chairs next to the one my bikini was on, and he grabs one and hands it to me.

I groan as I sit up. "I should get home. I have to open tomorrow."

"What time do you have to be there?"

"Five." I wrap myself in the towel. Now that Alexander isn't on top of me, goosebumps appear on my skin.

"Shit," he mutters, grabbing his phone from his pocket. "It's just after three."

Sighing, I pad over to my dress. I knew it'd be a late night, but not *this* late. At this rate, there's not even a point in me trying to get in a nap. And yet, I'm not even annoyed. Watching Alexander as he gets dressed, I can't help but think that tonight was worth it.

"I'll drive you." He doesn't bother buttoning his shirt, just leaves it hanging open. His wet hair is tousled, dripping onto the fabric.

I dress quickly, wishing I brought a jacket. "I can grab a cab or something. You must be tired."

"Absolutely not. I want to make sure you get home safe."

I pause as I pull on my heels, resisting the smile that's tugging at my lips. The urge to let this become more than a one-time thing is strong. But I'm not stupid enough to let myself make that decision right now. Not right after we had sex. However much I want him to rip off my clothes and fuck me again, I know I need some objectivity.

The ride home is mostly silent. Alexander turns on the heat almost immediately, saying something about not wanting me to catch a cold.

I watch as the buildings around us turn from luxury homes to a shopping district to middle class homes, and then finally into my neighborhood. I'm grateful for the darkness that hides my reddening cheeks.

I wonder if it's a weird feeling for Alexander, knowing that he just fucked me in his multi-million dollar mansion, only to drop me off at a house that's literally falling apart. If it bugs him, he doesn't show it.

After he parks in front of the house, he turns and pulls me in for a kiss. "Thank you for tonight, Sophia." There's a longing it his voice that sends a pang of guilt through me.

Did I just use him for a fun night and sex? Did we use each other?

But as I look into his eyes, I see that darkness there, mixed with a desire so strong it makes me jerk back. How can he be this intense after we've been up all night?

"I don't want to lose you, Soph. *I'm not going to lose you again.*"

I stare at him silently, gripping the edge of my seat. Because I'm not his to lose. And I'm not entirely sure I want to be. So I wish him a good night, kiss him on the cheek, and practically run into the house.

Once the front door is closed and locked, I lean against it and let out a breath.

I'm not going to lose you again.

Glancing out the window in the door, I watch as Alexander's car pulls away. Relief floods me, but a bit of disappointment follows.

Do I want to see him again? Do I want to let this happen? Will I regret it if I do? Biting my lip, I turn away as his car leaves my sight.

Most importantly, do I trust him enough to believe this is real?

CHAPTER 2

Sophia

"I just don't know how I feel about all of this," I tell Lissa. I'm at the coffee shop, re-stocking the cups and lids before we open.

Alexander came back to pick me up, practically shoving a breakfast smoothie into my hands. It was kind, and I'm grateful I didn't have to deal with public transportation today. But I don't want him to get too attached.

"You shouldn't've told him this was a one-time thing." Lissa is leaning against the counter, giving me a playful glare. "He seems really into you."

"*Too* into me," I mutter under my breath. Sure, I never really got over Alexander. But I certainly haven't obsessed over him for the past five years.

"Why are you so closed off to giving this a shot?"

I pause, a sleeve of medium cups hanging from my hand. A part of me wants to tell Lissa everything, about how magical it was to be in his arms, about how his father hated mine for some reason. How I gave Alexander my heart, just for him to shatter it the same way his father shattered my father.

But I can't get into all of that right now. My heart can't re-live that pain again.

So I just say, "He broke my heart. I don't know if I trust him."

Lissa makes a low sound, signaling that she understands.

For the next half hour, we work in silence. I can't get the feel of Alexander out of my head. The way he touched me. Filled me. Tore me apart.

The morning drags by, and I down coffee after coffee to keep myself upright. When Brent comes in, I realize I've forgotten to make his drink.

I ring him out. "Sorry, it'll just be a few minutes."

"No worries. I'm a bit early today." He smiles at me from across the counter as he swipes his card. His soft brown eyes glint in the sunlight, holding my gaze. For a second, he looks like he's going to say something else, but then he steps back with a small nod.

I glance at the clock on the wall. It's 9:55. "Damn. Proud of you." I shoot him a smile as I grab a cup to pour his coffee.

The little bell on the front door rings as I hand Brent his cup. Our fingers brush, and he pauses, catching my gaze again.

"I hope you have a lovely day, Sophia," he says softly. Sincerely. And then he turns, bumping into a tall, stiff figure on his way out.

Alexander.

A scowl is etched onto his face, and he glares after Brent.

Irritation flashes through me. "Why do you hate him so much? He's a nice guy."

Alexander's gaze cuts to mine, still hard, but without hate. "I detest any man who looks at you for longer than he has to."

I snort, and I hear Lissa let out a small giggle behind me.

"Do you want your usual?" I try to keep my voice tense, but the second I look at him, everything inside me softens.

"Please."

I quickly pour him a black coffee and shove it into his hands. "Two dollars."

He already has his wallet in his hands, and he pulls out a bill and sets it on the counter. "Keep the change." With that, he turns on his heel and stalks out.

"Fucking hell," Lissa whispers as she steps up next to me.

We both stare at the hundred-dollar bill sitting on the counter. It ignites so many different emotions in me. Anger. Gratitude. Suspicion.

Is he flaunting his wealth in front of me, reminding me what could be mine if I let myself fall for him again? Did guilt finally overtake him after dropping me off at my house? Or is he trying to buy me? Because he fucking can't.

"We're gonna split that, right?" Lissa says as I open the register and put the bill in the empty slot for bigger bills.

Yanking $98 out, I say, "You can have it all," before shoving it into her hands and storming outside.

"Alexander!" I shout, crossing the sidewalk to him.

He's watching me, leaning against his sleek, gray car and sipping his coffee calmly.

"You can't buy me," I snap.

"I don't need to, little bird."

I bristle at the use of my pet name. It may have had me begging for him last night, but now? Now it feels manipulative. Demeaning.

"You don't own me." I shove at him, but he barely moves. "And I don't need you."

He hums, taking another sip and smiling smugly. His eyes are dark. Predatory. "That's not what you said last night. If I recall correctly, you were begging for me."

I stumble backward as his words hit me. "That was a mistake. All of this has been a mistake."

He closes the space between us, pulling me close with his free hand. "Go ahead. Run. You know I've always loved the chase."

"Fuck off," I yell.

"Is that what you want?" He pulls me closer, until I can feel his heart pounding through his chest. "*Really.* Or is that what you want to want?"

My breath hitches as his lips brush my cheekbone.

"I know you, Sophia," he whispers in my ear. "I can read you like a book, remember? And you want me to shove you into the nearest alley and rip your clothes off, tie you up with this little apron, and then fuck you until the whole city hears your screams."

I can feel my cheeks heating, and while heat might also be pooling between my legs, my mind is reeling with anger. "Do you think I'm stupid? That I'd really fall for you again? You broke me, Xander. *Broke* me. And I'm not going to let you do it again."

His face fills with fury. "You think I wanted to—"

"Sophia? Are you okay?"

I turn to see Brent standing a few feet away, a concerned look on his face.

"I heard you yelling, so I turned back." He's standing straight, puffing out his chest a bit. He's not tiny, but he's definitely not big—and no match for Alexander.

"I'm fine." I pull away, but his grip on me tightens. "Fuck off, Xander."

"Let her go, man." Brent steps closer.

The two of them glare at each other, and for a second I begin to think that the air between them is going to spontaneously combust into flames. But then Alexander releases me.

"This conversation isn't over, Sophia." His tone is smooth as he moves to the other side of his car and slides in.

I let out a breath, but then jump at the feel of a hand on my shoulder. *Brent.*

"Are you okay?" His brows are furrowed as he glances between me and Alexander's car pulling away from the curb.

I nod, brushing a few stray hairs out of my face. "He's just an ass. I shouldn't've come out here. Thanks for turning back."

He lets out a little chuckle. "The one time I was going to make it to work on time."

"Fuck. Brent, I'm so sor-"

"Don't." He gives me a warm smile and squeezes my arm before letting go. "You're worth it. You'll be okay back inside?"

My body relaxes. *Compassion.* That's what Alexander seems to lack. And it's so comforting to see it in Brent's eyes. "Yeah, I'll be fine. Thanks."

With another smile, he heads off, and I slip back inside. Lissa scrambles away from the window where she was watching.

"That looked intense," she says. "I see why you're uneasy."

"Uneasy barely describes how I feel." I grab the broom from the back and start sweeping the dining room. It may not need it, but I need the distraction. "I don't think I ever want to see him again."

Lissa is silent for a moment, then shrugs and heads to the back to do up the dishes.

Thankfully, the day goes by quickly. I get off at two and decide to walk home instead of waiting for the bus. It's not a terribly long walk, and I need to clear my head.

When Alexander came back to take me to work this morning, I felt a mixture of pleasure and dread. Pleasure because I've missed him. What we had. Because his hands on my body last night were the best thing I've felt in ages.

But the dread is what ate at me during the short drive to work. The feeling that he's using me, and he'll drop me the second I become inconvenient.

Just like last time.

By the time I'm home, all I want to do is shower and collapse into bed for twelve hours. Rachel and Victoria aren't home, so I have the bathroom to myself.

I turn on the water and strip out of my clothes, avoiding looking at myself in the mirror. I know I probably look terrible.

When I step into the shower, I let out a hiss. Our water heater broke a few days ago, and our landlord isn't answering his goddamn phone.

I wash my hair and scrub my body quickly, and when I exit the shower, I'm covered in goosebumps. After toweling myself off, I pull on a hoodie and some shorts, and then jump under my covers.

Despite the sunlight streaming through my windows, sleep overtakes me, even as my mind reels with anger.

Fuck our water heater. Fuck today. And fuck Alexander.

. . .

My memories come back to haunt me in my sleep.

He's driving, with a hand on my leg, dangerously close to slipping up my skirt. We're laughing, happy to be free from school for the day.

And then a car pulls out in front of us, and the sickening sound of glass shattering and metal crunching reverberates in my ears.

I taste blood.

"Soph-Sophia, are you okay?" He's reaching for me, wiping blood off my lip, always taking care of me before himself.

And then he's gone, yanked out of the car. He struggles, but it doesn't matter.

I scream as the gun lets loose, wishing I could turn away, wishing I didn't have to lose him again.

. . .

"Sophia!"

I wake to a hand on my shoulder, shaking me. Rachel.

I jump, gasping for air. There are tears in my eyes.

It's dark, and according to my clock, it's a little after ten.

"You okay?"

I let my body relax and fall back into my pillows. *It was just a dream. It's over. It doesn't matter anymore.* "I'm fine. What do you need?"

"There's some dude waiting for you downstairs. He's super hot."

"Tell him to fuck off," I grumble, burrowing into my pillow.

"Uh-uh, Soph. You've rejected too many great guys. I'm not letting you blow this chance!" She grabs my covers and yanks, exposing my legs.

I shriek as the cold air hits my skin. "Seriously?!"

"Get up, brush your teeth, and do something with your hair. I'm not sending him away, so you'll have to do it yourself. And you definitely don't want to do it looking like you do right now." Her voice is playful, but there's a bit of concern in her eyes.

"Fine."

"Good." Rachel leaves, but not before flipping on the light and blinding me.

"Fuck you," I yell, shutting my eyes. But I know she means well, and I need to get this conversation over with anyway.

After freshening up and realizing there's nothing I can do about my bloodshot eyes, I head downstairs. Alexander is in the entryway, and I hate the feeling of relief that hits me when I see him there, alive. Not bleeding out.

Blinking back more tears, I greet him with a small nod, staying on the bottom step of the stairs. I've got to shake off the dream. It was years ago. He's not mine to lose anymore.

"Are you here to apologize?" I cross my arms.

"I told you I'm not going to lose you again, Sophia."

I bite my lip. Then a shadow of movement catches my attention, and I see eyes peering through the crack in the dining room door.

"I can see you," I say, glaring at Rachel and Victoria.

They slink into the room, both giving Alexander shy smiles. "We're just curious about your mystery man, Soph."

I sigh. "This is . . . Alexander."

Victoria gasps. "THE Alexander? Like, your ex?! Oh my god, are you guys getting back together?"

I groan.

"This is perfect," Rachel exclaims, clasping her hands together. "She never got over you, dude. Sometimes I hear her screaming your name in the middle of the night."

"RACHEL!" I cover my reddening face, wishing I could just disappear. "I regret ever telling either of you anything about my personal life."

The girls squeal, telling Alexander that he's the ex I talk about the most. That I've always said he was the best kisser.

"Enough," I shout.

A satisfied smirk rests on Alexander's face. But he turns to the girls. "We could use some privacy." Then he turns back to me. "How about a walk."

Spending time alone with Alexander is the last thing I want to do, but some movement will probably help the heavy weight in my chest to dissipate. So I grab my flip-flops and head outside with him.

We walk in silence, heading to a small park a few blocks away. I don't know what to say, and either Alexander is in the same boat, or he's waiting for me to initiate.

I try to focus on the way the night air feels on my skin, or how this neighborhood doesn't look quite as rundown in the dark. How the silent streets are oddly comforting.

Finally, we reach the park, and Alexander stops us under a streetlight.

His gaze glides over my body as he raises an eyebrow. "That hoodie isn't helping your case."

I look down, barely remembering what I slipped on before collapsing into bed. It's a soft gray fabric, with our high school's logo on the back. On the front, just above my heart, is Alexander's embroidered name.

Fuck.

He'd let me borrow this hoodie a few nights before he broke my heart and left me sobbing behind our school. It's still too big on me, but the practical side of me that knows I always get cold wouldn't let me get rid of it.

Although that isn't the only reason I've kept it.

"It's not what you think."

"Screaming my name in the middle of the night? C'mon."

A chill runs down my spine, and as if on cue, tears spring to my eyes. "Also not what you think." My voice is scratchy, and I hate the lump that appeared so easily in my throat.

Alexander's face falls. "Oh, fuck. Soph."

I've screamed Alexander's name plenty of times out of tortured pleasure. But there was one time when it was because of something else—a fear that gripped my heart so tightly I thought it would explode.

We were seventeen, leaving school to go hang out with some of our friends. But we never made it. A vehicle cut us off on the road, causing us to crash. And then a group of men came from out of nowhere, wrenching the car door open and pulling Alexander out at gunpoint. Leaving me behind.

It took his father a week to negotiate with his kidnappers on the price of the ransom. He saw nothing wrong with gambling with his son's life to try to save a few million.

A shiver runs through me. Whenever I'm stressed, that crash finds a way back into my dreams, and it always ends with Xander lying on the ground, lifeless, blood seeping from his body.

Gone, forever.

I cover my mouth to stifle a sob. In a single movement, Alexander pulls me close to him, wrapping his arms around me and pressing his lips to the top of my head.

I don't even try to resist. The part of me that's still shaken from my nightmare needs this reassurance that he's still alive, that he made it out in one piece. That he came back to me—even if it was just to leave me later.

"How often?" he asks.

It takes me a moment to realize what he means—how often I still have nightmares about his kidnapping. About almost losing him.

"Once or twice a month, usually. Whenever I'm stressed, or I see something that reminds me of it."

He holds me tighter. "I didn't think it would still affect you that much."

I stiffen. "Why, because you left me?" Anger rises in my chest, replacing the deep sorrow that's haunted me for years. I shove away from him, stumbling backward.

"Because I didn't think you still cared."

His words pierce me like a knife. Because he saw how heartbroken I was. How I was a lifeless shell for the rest of senior year.

"If I recall correctly, you were always the heartless one," I say flatly.

He reaches for me, but I bat his hand away. Anger flashes through his eyes, but it's gone in an instant. With a deep breath, he says, "I was trying to protect you."

"Protect me? From what? You ruined me. You tore me into pieces. I was willing to leave everything for you, Alexander. I was yours. And you *left*."

He grabs me, and when I resist, he just holds me tighter. "You think I wanted to leave you? You think I wasn't torn up just as much? I loved you, Sophia Aswall, and I'll never fucking stop."

"Then why?" I shout. "Why did you leave me?"

He claps a hand over my mouth. "Calm down. People are sleeping."

I glare up at him, waiting for a response. But he doesn't give one. He just glares back.

For a moment, I care. I give him the benefit of the doubt and tell myself he wouldn't leave me without a good reason. But I dash the hope rising up in me in an instant.

Because it can't be true. It doesn't make sense, and we both know it.

Yanking his hand away, I say, "You don't get to destroy me, abandon me for five years, and then swoop back into my life and think I'll fall into your arms because you're a good fuck."

His grip on me loosens ever so slightly, and I use it to squirm out of his arms.

"Sophia, don't do this." His eyes are dark, threatening. Just like they were this morning at the coffee shop.

"Either give me answers, or get the fuck out of my life."

His jaw clenches, and I can see him struggling to lock up his fury in a little box.

Good. He doesn't own me, and he needs to know it.

"My father forced my hand. Either I broke up with you, or he was going to ship me off to a boarding school for the rest of senior year. So I chose to at least be near you, even if I couldn't have you."

I snort. "And then we barely saw each other after graduation."

"Sophia—"

"No! I don't believe you. Your father couldn't control you after you turned eighteen. You always talked about getting out from under his thumb as soon as you could. So what the fuck changed, Alexander?" I'm slowly backing away from him, watching his anger morph into pain.

"It was best for my family at the time. For my mother."

I roll my eyes. "You think that's going to convince me? I'm not going to be with someone who'll choose his mother over me."

He takes a step forward. "That's fair, and I agree. But the threat that forced me to choose between her and you is gone now."

"Until something else comes up. I was obviously too inconvenient to fight for last time."

He bristles. "Don't say that."

"Then prove me wrong." My entire body is shaking, and pressure is building behind my eyes. *I can't cry. Not now. Not like this.*

"You're cold." He takes off his jacket and steps toward me.

I stumble backward, knowing that if he touches me, I'll be done for. But my foot catches on a crack in the sidewalk, and I fall backwards.

As if he predicted it would happen, Alexander rushes toward me and catches me right before I hit the ground. He pulls me up, holding me as I regain my balance.

"Sophia, I've already told you more than once. I'm not losing you again. Trust me or don't trust me, I don't give a fuck. You're *mine*. And I'm not leaving you alone until you know it."

My breath catches, and even though I know it'll do no good, I struggle against him. I'm met with a wall of muscle and arms of steel. "You don't deserve a second chance," I snap.

"I never said I did."

I stop struggling, looking up at him in shock. "Then what—"

"What I deserve doesn't change the fact that you're mine. Whether you decide to give me another chance doesn't change a thing. I'm in your life, Sophia. Permanently."

My hands clutch at the sleeves of his shirt as I glare up at him. This *asshole.* He's not even giving me a choice.

Either I willingly give him a second chance, or he'll take one by force. Take *me* by force—my heart, my soul, my body.

The possessiveness in his eyes should scare me, but instead it tugs at something deep inside of me. Something that wants to surrender to him.

I shove that part of me down. No matter what he's saying, Alexander is trouble. And I have to stay in control as much as I possibly can.

His arms tighten around my waist, waiting for my response. Getting impatient.

Two choices.

Condemn myself to fighting him off until he relents—if he ever does.

Or give him the damn chance. Give it to him, give myself a bit of control over this contorted version of a relationship, and keep my guard up.

I'll find a way out of this somehow.

Unless things work out.

My whole body goes still at the thought.

There isn't a safe way to entangle myself with Alexander. No matter how hard I try, a small part of me will always hope. Hope that he means it. That he won't lose me again. Won't leave me again.

But it's not worth the risk. This is going to blow up in my face—I know it.

I'm not going to lose you again.

I shut my eyes, shaking my head at the way his words get under my skin. I won't open up to him. I won't let him in.

I'm not getting my heart broken again.

His lips brush against mine, and he lets out a low groan. "You're running out of time, little bird."

Fuck. Fuck, fuck, fuck. His breath mingles with mine as he presses me into his body. The place that I once considered my safest, most sacred place. My home.

My everything.

I press my lips to his, wrapping my arms around his neck. But after a moment, he pulls away.

"No. Say it." His eyes are hard, his lips pressed into a thin line.

"I'll give you a chance," I whisper.

Those words seem to unlock something inside him. His hand wraps around the back of my neck as his mouth descends on mine.

This kiss is different from the ones last night. It's hungrier, more unhinged. As he thrusts his tongue into my mouth, I realize how much he was holding back.

And then his hands are on my ass, and my feet lift off the ground. Instinctively, I wrap my legs around his waist and kiss him harder, lightly biting his bottom lip. He lets out something between a moan and a growl, slamming my back against the lamppost.

"Do you remember the last time I saw you in this hoodie?" he says after pulling away ever so slightly.

"A party at your parent's house, outside by the fire. You let me wear it because I was cold."

"And then what?" His voice is rough, his fingers digging into my ass cheeks so hard I wonder if I'll have bruises there tomorrow.

"You kept me outside until everyone left. On your lap. You kept leaving little kisses on my neck." I shudder as he does so now, his lips shooting sparks under my skin.

"And then I fucked you in the grass next to the dying embers. You looked entirely too adorable in this hoodie. I needed to ruin you." A hand slides under the soft fabric, gripping my waist.

I run my fingers through his hair and kiss him fiercely. There's no way I can fight the want—the *need*—building up inside me right now. I'll get it under control later.

"You can't wear this hoodie and expect me to not tear it off of you." His hand slides up further, cupping my breast as his thumb runs across my nipple.

"Alexander," I gasp. "We're in public."

It may be the middle of the night, but someone could still drive by. And a few houses still have some lights on.

"That makes you wet, doesn't it?"

I squirm in his arms. He's right and he knows it. But still—what if we get caught? What if I can't control my screams?

His hand slips out from underneath my shirt and holds me closer. And then we're moving, into the park and under the cover of a few trees. He sets me on a picnic table, not wasting any time before yanking the hoodie over my head.

The cool air hits my skin, and I shiver at the absence of the fabric keeping me warm. He moves to pull off my shorts and underwear, but then stops.

A hand cups my chin, and I look up at him. He leans down and kisses me, and this time it's not hungry or fierce. It's slow, patient. Like he has all the time in the world to explore me.

And maybe he does.

Fingers slide down my spine, then back up again, before gripping the hair at the back of my head. He holds me still while his lips move against mine and his tongue runs across my bottom lip.

I try to move my head up to kiss him harder, but his grip on my hair tightens as he holds me in place.

"Not yet, little bird." His breath on my face is warm, and I let out a small whimper. I can feel myself aching for him, needing him.

But he continues his slow exploration, planting kisses on my cheeks, my nose, my jaw. Finally, he reaches my neck and sucks lightly, tilting my head back to give him more room.

"You're perfect," he mumbles against my skin. His kisses fall onto my shoulders and collarbone. "A goddess."

He sucks the spot between my breasts, and I groan, arching my back. One of my hands slides in between my legs, but he slaps it away.

"Did I tell you that you could touch yourself?" He pulls away, and I instantly crave the little bit of heat he was giving me. "You're *mine*. And your little cunt is for my hands only."

"Then take me." I grip his arms, panting as he looks down at me. Even in the dark, I can see the glint of passion in his eyes.

He lets out a breath, not looking away as he shoves a hand down the front of my shorts. His fingers slide over my folds easily. "You're soaked."

He brushes over my clit, and a shudder runs through me. And then he's tearing off the rest of my clothes and kneeling on the ground, kissing my inner thighs.

When his tongue finally circles my clit, I bite my lip to stifle my moan. I can't tell what exactly he's doing, but it's sending slivers of pleasure through my entire body.

He thrusts three fingers into me, curling them against the walls of my vagina. One of my hands props me up on the table, and the other is grabbing a fistful of his hair.

I'm on the edge, and just before he pushes me over, he pulls away, his fingers sliding out of me. He shoves them into his mouth and licks himself clean.

"Do you want me, Sophia?"

I'm still reeling from the absence of his touch, my body coming down from my almost-orgasm. All I can manage is a little nod.

"You do, don't you? Tell me how badly you want me."

"I need you," I pant, sitting up so I can look at him better. "It's more than wanting. I need you, Xander."

Alarms sound in the back of my head, telling me that's a stupid thing to say. That I shouldn't need him.

I ignore them.

"What do you need me to do?" He begins kissing my inner thighs again.

"Fuck me," I whisper. My legs are shaking.

"Louder."

"Fuck me."

"*Louder.*"

"Fuck me," I shout, not caring who hears the desperation in my words.

Alexander lets out a low growl as he rips open his belt, undoing his pants and pulling his cock out. He's already rock hard.

But he doesn't slam into me, no matter how much I want him to. No matter how much I know *he* wants to. Instead, he spreads my legs apart, positioning himself at my entrance. Then he rolls his hips forward, slowly entering me.

His gaze is locked in with mine as I silently beg him to take me, to overpower me. But he continues with his slow pace, not looking away from me.

"I want this to last, Sophia. I've missed you so much."

"So have I." The words rush out of my mouth before I even have a chance to think.

He leans down and kisses me, one of his hands squeezing my breast. While I moan at his touch, he continues his slow pace. I let myself get lost in the rhythm of it. Of him.

He kisses my lips one last time before moving down to suck one of my nipples into his mouth. He moans, driving himself into me harder, and I raise my hips to meet him.

"God, Sophia." He straightens. Still tweaking my nipple between his fingers, he picks up his pace.

I let out a whimper in response. His finger brushes against my clit, causing my body to jerk, but he works me lightly until the discomfort turns back into pleasure.

His eyes don't leave mine as he thrusts as hard as he can, filling me. I dig my nails into his arms, grinding against him.

It's everything I've missed in the men who came after him. Everything I've craved for years and told myself I'd never find again.

But with him here, one hand wrapping around my throat, the other stroking my clit, I can't help but let myself hope.

The world fades around us, and my focus falls onto Alexander. The way his hair is a mess from my fingers. How his muscles bulge through his shirt. His fingers, holding me in place, not even needing to use any force.

In this moment—this blissful, perfect moment—I'm completely his.

When I come, it's with a cry that echoes throughout the park. He follows soon after, and I watch as his body tightens, stills, and then collapses onto me.

We lay there, and I gaze up at the few stars glistening in the sky. The steady feeling of Alexander's heartbeat calms me, and I wrap my arms around him.

After a few minutes of peaceful quiet, he pulls out of me, leaving a trail of kisses down my body before he straightens and pulls his pants back up.

I find my underwear and shorts, fully remembering that we're in the middle of a park. The trees and darkness only offer a certain amount of cover.

Goosebumps are covering my arms as Alexander pulls my hoodie over my head. My hand slides up his chest, and he pulls me into a soft, warm kiss.

With multiple layers of clothing between us, I'm gaining my senses again. Part of me wants to hold him close and tell him that I'm his, forever. But the smart side of me knows that's a recipe for disaster.

We walk back to the house in silence, my hand in his. He doesn't come back inside—just leaves me with a kiss before walking back to his car in darkness.

I watch him go from the entryway's window, still feeling his cum leaking out of me.

The house is quiet, so I assume the girls have gone to bed. It's for the best. I don't work at the coffee shop until tomorrow morning, but I have some client work I need to get done. And since I just slept for almost eight hours, I can't pass up this time to get some writing done.

Hell, I can't pass up *any* time to get some writing done. If I want to make enough money to be able to quit my day job, I need to keep myself focused on building up my little business.

So I head up to my room, open up my laptop, and write until around two. By then, I'm having trouble keeping my eyes open, so I let myself take a short nap.

Thankfully, I don't dream.

CHAPTER 3

Sophia

The shop is busy this morning, keeping Lissa and me on our toes. When Brent walks in, I barely even realize that he's early again.

Finally getting it together, huh?

My stomach flutters. I can't deny that responsibility is an attractive trait. I've always thought Brent is pretty cute, but I've been telling myself for months that I just don't have time for a boyfriend right now.

And then Alexander swooped in and barely gave me a choice.

For a moment, I let myself think back to how he felt inside of me last night, telling me that he'd missed me—and how I'd said it back without hesitation.

Brent clears his throat, and I realize I'm standing behind the counter, staring out the window with his coffee in my hand.

"Right! Sorry. Here you go. Proud of you for being early again. I won't keep you this time." I flash him a quick smile while I ring him out.

He steps away from the counter, but his eyes stay trained on me. "Like I said, you're worth it. That guy seems like an asshole. Is he . . . giving you trouble?"

I shake my head. This isn't the time for the truth. "We were just fighting last night. It's complicated."

Just then, the door opens again, and I don't even have to look over before I know it's Alexander. It's almost like I can *feel* him.

Apparently, the same isn't true for Brent. He pauses for a moment before saying, "So you're not single?"

Shit. I open my mouth to say something, but I barely have a chance.

Alexander walks past Brent, beelining for the counter. "Good morning, sweetheart. Sleep well?" He reaches for me, pulling me until my hips hit the counter. After planting a kiss on my lips, he pulls away and smiles.

"I—uh—I slept a little bit after—" I clamp my mouth shut before admitting to the whole shop that Alexander completely railed me last night.

"Do you get off at two again?"

"Uh—four."

"I'll pick you up then." With that, Alexander flashes me a charming smile before turning on his heel and walking out.

Without even ordering.

I'm left with my mouth slightly open, barely registering the quiet giggle coming from Lissa. I catch Brent's gaze, and he nods at me, his lips pressed into a thin line.

Then he leaves, too.

Shit, shit, shit.

Sure, I'm with Alexander. Sort of. But I like Brent. And before Alexander came along, I'd been thinking about asking him out.

Now? If things don't work out with Alexander and I end up with Brent, what does that make him? A backup plan? Even if that isn't how I plan it, that's probably how Brent would feel.

I turn around, trying to bury my fury. Drive thru is backed up, and Lissa and I need to get it caught up before the next rush. So I dive in, momentarily forgetting about the stunt that Alexander just pulled.

When we finally have a break, Lissa shoots me a look. "Those two looked ready to kill each other."

"I didn't notice," I say, grabbing a couple sleeves of cups to restock. It's an obvious lie, but thankfully she doesn't point it out.

"Soooo you were with him last night?" Lissa wiggles her eyebrows at me.

I turn away as a blush creeps onto my cheeks. "Maybe he stopped by."

"And?"

I pause. How much do I want to tell her? Definitely not about the sex. "He . . . Uh, he just wanted to apologize for yesterday morning. We just talked." I grit my teeth. He actually *hasn't* apologized, and I've forgotten about it until now.

"That's good. He looked a little crazed out there." She sighs. "Poor Brent. I think he really likes you."

Cringing, I say, "I feel so bad. Now it looks like I led him on."

Lissa gives me a sympathetic smile. She's watched me flirt with him little by little, and she's been trying to get me to ask him out for ages.

And I put it off, thinking I had all the time in the world to get around to it.

"Alexander asked me to give him another chance." *Sort of.*

Lissa freezes, one hand on the broom. Waiting for me to continue.

"I said yes." Turning, I realize there are tears in my eyes. "And I'm really scared, Lissa. I don't want to get hurt again."

That part is true. If last night is any indication of how our relationship is going to go, I'm fucked. I lose all sense when he puts his hands on me. My heart is vulnerable, unprotected.

I *have* to change that.

"Oh, babe." She lets the broom fall and clank against a cooler. Pulling me into her arms, she mutters, "Heartbreak is a motherfucker. Are you sure you want to do this?"

"I don't know," I say, sniffling. "And I don't know what *he* wants. If he truly means it when he says that he wants to be with me no matter what."

"Why do you think he's worth another shot?"

I pause. Last night, I told Alexander that he didn't deserve a second chance, and I meant it. But I'd be lying to Lissa *and* myself if I say his touch doesn't entirely unravel me.

Lissa pulls away, looking me hard in the eyes. "Well?"

Letting out a breath, I say, "Because he feels like coming home. He's infuriating, but he's comforting. We were so good together before he broke up with me."

She gives my arm a squeeze. "Well, those aren't terrible reasons. Just be careful, okay? There's nothing wrong with keeping your guard up until you're sure you can trust him."

I nod, blinking back my tears.

I just don't know if I can.

. . .

My shift drags on, and when 4 o'clock finally hits, I'm ready to get home. We've been short-staffed, and while I don't mind the overtime, eleven hour shifts are the worst.

I wave goodbye to Lissa before heading out. I'll get home faster if I walk, but taking the bus means I can get off my aching feet.

I turn to head for the bus stop but freeze when I see Alexander leaning against his car. I completely forgot he said he'd pick me up.

The anger I felt this morning rises in my chest. But he pushes off the car, planting a kiss on my cheek and taking my bag. When he opens the passenger door, I glare at him.

"You don't own me," I snap. "What you did this morning? That was fucked up. You don't need to get under Brent's skin like that."

Alexander's lips quirk up in a devilish smile. "I told you. I hate any man who looks at you for longer than he has to."

"Well, keep it bottled up." I shove at his chest, but he catches my wrists, holding them so my hands are pressed to his chest. "If you're going to be an ass, this whole thing is off."

He leans down, saying lowly in my ear, "We can do this the easy way, little bird. Or you can make this harder on both of us."

I let out a huff, but when he opens the passenger side door, I slide in.

When he's settled in the driver's seat, he gives me a quick glance before saying, "Have you eaten today?"

I close my eyes, too pissed and tired to meet his gaze. We were so busy today that we barely got a break. All I've had today was a little snack around one.

"Sort of." But my traitorous stomach growls at the mere thought of eating a meal.

"You need food." His voice is stern as he pulls out of his parking spot.

I don't argue, just keeping my eyes closed in silence. I'm too exhausted to even look at him.

We drive for a while, the warmth of the sun shining through the windows lulling me into a light sleep. But a stop at a red light pulls me back into consciousness.

I turn my head to look at Alexander. His hands are both on the steering wheel, his gaze locked on the car in front of us. His jaw is tense, but not in the way that indicates he's upset. This is just his normal level of tension.

The way he'd held me still, telling me we could do this his way or the hard way, floats through my memory. I hate that he has almost all the upper ground.

"You don't own me," I mumble sleepily.

He chuckles, giving me a quick glance as the car in front of us moves.

"I mean it." I adjust myself so I'm facing him more, but my eyelids are threatening to close again. "Brent is a nice guy. I was going to ask him out before you crashed back into my life."

"I'm *so* sorry," he says with obvious sarcasm. His grip on the steering wheel is tighter, and he works his jaw. *Now* he's pissed.

"Look, I'm giving you a chance. But that doesn't mean you get to just fuck up my life because some guy makes you jealous. I like him. And I don't know what's going to happen between us. So leave him alone."

"I've already told you. I'm not losing you again, Sophia."

"That's what *you* want. But I don't trust you, Alexander, and you can't expect me to."

His nostrils flare, but he stays quiet, brooding. Because he knows I'm right. I have no reason to blindly give him my trust—he practically admitted it last night.

I look out the window. The surrounding buildings look vaguely familiar, but I'm not sure why. "Where are we going?"

"You'll see." His voice is low, dark.

"Xander, I'm exhausted, and I'm still in my uniform. I don't want to do anything right now except shower and sleep for the next decade. Where are you taking me?"

"Just trust—" he cuts himself off, exhaling sharply. "I'm just getting you some food, and then I'm taking you home."

Sighing, I settle against the seat. Wherever we're going seems annoyingly out of the way, but whatever. I can sleep in the car. So I close my eyes again, and soon enough, reality starts to bend and meld with my fleeting dreams.

When Alexander's hand brushes against my leg, I jump awake.

"Where are we?" I mumble, looking around. We're in a familiar-looking parking lot, and when I glance up at the building in front of us, something inside me warms.

Café Luna.

We used to come here all the time when we were in high school. It was a bit of a drive, but I loved their summer berry salad.

"I'll be right back." He plants a kiss on my forehead before heading inside the café, leaving the car running.

My eyes flutter closed again, but I don't let myself fall back asleep. I can't. A smile is creeping onto my face, and I can't stop it.

He remembered. It's been years since we've come here together, but he remembered.

Because he cares.

My shoulders tense at the thought, and I brush it off. I can't project extra feelings and intentions onto Alexander. I can't let myself get caught up in this.

He hasn't earned your trust yet, Sophia. He won't. Don't you dare give it to him.

In a few minutes, he comes back with a takeout bag in one hand and a drink in the other. Once he's opened the door, he hands me both. "Frozen lemonade and summer berry salad with grilled chicken, no dressing."

I take both, mumbling a thank you. To hide the smile still plastered onto my face, I keep my head down, focusing on opening up the salad container and diving in.

It tastes just how I remember, the perfect blend of fruits covering up the bitterness of the greens. I'm probably halfway through when I realize Alexander hasn't started driving yet.

"What?" I say, setting down the fork.

He's watching me, his dark brown eyes full of passion and restrained want. But he just shakes his head and turns away, backing up and then pulling out of the parking lot.

Shrugging, I continue to eat. I'm too hungry to continue our conversation, and honestly, I don't want to. I know I hurt him by telling him I don't trust him, but it's nothing he doesn't already know.

Still. I know I'd be devastated if someone I loved said those words to me. But I don't love him, and he doesn't love me. We've barely seen each other in years.

And he hasn't even apologized yet.

I settle back as I finish my salad. That's an argument for another time.

When Alexander parks in front of my house, I undo my seatbelt and lean over to give him a quick kiss him on the cheek. He places a hand on the back of my neck, keeping me near him, and presses his lips to mine.

"Thank you for the food," I say in between kisses. "And the ride."

"I'll pick you up tomorrow, too."

I sit back. "You don't have to."

"I *want* to. That way I know you get to and from work safe. And I know it's easier on you, as well."

I snort. "You want to pick me up at a quarter to five every morning?"

"So what if I do?"

My toes curl in my shoes. This is all going too fast. "Look, I get that you're trying to prove yourself, but—"

"This has nothing to do with that, and everything to do with your wellbeing. You walked out of the coffee shop today, and I barely recognized you. You're exhausted. If I pick you up in the mornings, you'll be able to sleep in more."

He's right, and I know it. I've been working myself so hard lately. *Too* hard. But I have bills to pay, and a writing career that I'm finally getting started. Neither of those things can wait.

Honestly, not having to catch the bus or walk to and from work *would* be really nice. It'd save me some time, and I'd be able to sleep in a bit more each morning.

"All right, fine." I grab my bag from the back, pausing to look at him. My heart softens when I find him watching me. "Thank you."

He kisses me. "I'll see you in the morning, Sophia."

CHAPTER 4

Sophia

For the next few days, Alexander picks me up without complaint, often with a homemade breakfast smoothie or my favorite salad in hand. It warms my heart, but it scares me at the same time.

On Friday, we're driving in silence, his hand resting on my leg. Music plays softly from the radio, and I'm about ready to fall asleep again. We were slammed today, and I'm starving.

Alexander's voice breaks the silence. "I have a gala tomorrow night. Charity thing. I need you to come with me."

His gaze is fixed ahead. If he's afraid of rejection, he's not showing it.

I bite my lip. I really need to work on my client's book. The deadline is approaching fast, and I want to put my best foot forward.

I haven't told Alexander about my client. It feels awkward, embarrassing. He's had his hands in some of the biggest tech companies in the country since before he even graduated high school. My little side hustle is barely surviving, and who knows if I'll be able to get a client after this one?

Writing has been my dream career since I was in high school. The fact that I'm just starting is embarrassing. And failing? That would be downright humiliating.

Which is why I haven't told a single soul—other than Lissa—and I'm not going to.

"I don't have a dress." It's a lame excuse, but it's true. Nothing I have would be fancy enough.

"I already bought you one." He's still looking ahead, almost stoic.

Anxiety curls in my stomach at the thought of being in a room full of people who are all more successful, more rich, and more put-together than I am.

But at the same time, it'd be nice to be seen with Alexander. To let everyone know that he's taken. I'm no fool—he had girls practically throwing themselves at him in high school. I highly doubt that's changed.

"I know it'll probably be a little awkward," he says. "There'll be some people there who'll recognize you. But I have no problem with leaving early if things get too uncomfortable for you."

My heart skips a beat. I hadn't even thought about that. How many of my old high school friends will be there? And what am I supposed to tell them when they ask me what I'm up to now? That I work in a coffee shop, live in a rundown house, and can barely make ends meet?

That I'm back together with the man who, five years previous, broke my heart? Broke *me?*

"That's . . . that's a lot, Xander."

He squeezes my leg. "I know. I promise I won't leave your side. And if you don't want to talk about yourself, I can help direct the conversation away from you. I just want you there."

I can't deny the relief that floods my chest at his words. But he's probably been to tons of these things by himself. Or with countless other dates.

A flare of jealousy shoots through me, and before I can stop myself, I say, "Why? Why me? Can't you go with someone else? Or your sister?"

He finally gives me a glance—fleeting but so focused it almost takes my breath away. "Because I want everyone to know that you're mine."

My heart warms, but it does nothing to ease the knots in my stomach. "I don't know, Alexander. It's been so long since I've been to one of these events. And it'll be so late by the time you drop me off."

"You'll be spending the night with me. I live close by."

I pick at a loose thread on my shirt. I've been able to keep Alexander at arm's length over the past week. It's not that I don't want him—in fact, it's the opposite. The force that I want him with scares me. And I need to keep things slow. I need to keep some tiny bit of control.

But it's not like this gala is some kind of commitment. And lots of couples spend the night together. Hell, some people even do it after a first date.

"Okay. But I'm holding you to your word. Don't you dare leave me by myself."

"I won't." His voice is firm, and I let myself believe him.

When he pulls up in front of my house, he has the car in park and his hands unbuckling my seatbelt before I've even reached for my bag. His lips crash against mine, his hand holding my head securely in place. It's like he just can't get enough of me.

"You need to pack a bag."

I barely register the words, too dumbfounded from his mind-numbing kiss. "What?"

"You're staying with me this weekend. I have meetings all morning tomorrow, but after that, I'm yours."

He peppers kisses along my cheekbone while I try to douse the fire igniting inside of me.

It doesn't work.

"I'm not your property," I manage. I jerk away from him, glaring into his stupidly-perfect brown eyes. "You can't just order me around like this."

His eyes cloud over, and with a twinge of regret, I realize what's coming. What I've set off.

His hand snakes around my throat. "You want to do this the hard way, little bird?"

I know I should back down. Bring my laptop, write during his meetings, and enjoy myself in his giant, luxurious house. But the thought of being that close to Alexander, for that long—I'd lose myself.

I'd forget that I'm *not* his. That he forced me into this. That I want out.

But my body refuses to cooperate, tensing instead of relaxing. Rebelling instead of giving in.

"That's kidnapping. I'll call the police."

Alexander laughs. Not mockingly, not bitterly.

He's *amused.*

"If you believe that I think it's beneath me to pay off a couple of police officers, you're wrong. Not to mention my public reputation is flawless. No one would ever believe that Philadelphia's golden boy would kidnap a girl like you. *Definitely* not the police."

"You're lying," I snap.

"Try me." He settles back into his seat, a smug look on his face.

This could be my way out. He kidnaps me, I file a restraining order, and then we're done. He literally *can't* be around me. So he can't force himself onto me.

But what if he's right? I can't deny that the Hendricks' name holds a lot of power around here. And it's no lie that most people would take Alexander's word over most women's.

As if he's reading my mind, Alexander says, "You can't get away from me, Sophia. So you might as well stop trying."

After a moment of silence, I say, "Is that what you want?"

His eyes narrow, and I know I have him right where I want him.

"Do you really just want me to surrender to you? To give up? To resign myself to a loveless, toxic future with you so you can control me?" I scoff, feeling satisfaction creep through me at the anger etched into his face. "At least I won't have to worry about money anymore. Just an asshole of a husband."

In a split second, he's in my face, stealing the air I breathe. "You can't weasel out of this, Sophia, and you can't manipulate me. You're *mine,* and the more you struggle against that concept, the harder things will be for you."

"So I won't struggle." I keep my voice cool, even though my heart is beating wildly in my chest. My body will always betray me whenever he invades my space. "But I won't be happy, either."

One of his hands grabs my upper thigh, and I try fruitlessly to squirm away.

"You see, I don't quite believe you." A finger traces over my throat, sending shivers through me as it drops below my collarbone.

A gasp escapes me as he pinches one of my nipples, hard.

"Part of you may always hate me, Sophia." He yanks my shirt up. "I can live with that. Because the rest of you? It craves me." His hand slides up my skin, resting over my heart.

My entire body is screaming, begging me to kiss him, to let him put his hands all over me. So when his hand slips underneath my bra, brushing against my sore nipple, I don't resist.

Fuck.

"Did you forget already that I can have you soaked and coming in mere minutes?" He bites the soft skin of my neck, tweaking my nipple in between two of his fingers.

A shiver runs through my body, and my legs open automatically at his hand pushing them apart. The logical, scared part of me is screaming at me to clamp them shut. To get out of this car and run inside, locking the door behind me.

But I stay still, trying to steady my breathing as his hands slowly tear down the walls I've tried so desperately to keep up.

"Take your shirt off." His words are curt, demanding.

"But someone could see." I glance out the car's windows before returning my gaze to his. The fire burning in them makes me obey, and I toss my shirt into the backseat.

He doesn't give me a single spare second before he's unclasping my bra, throwing it into the back, and grabbing both of my wrists. He pins them to the ceiling of the car.

His mouth descends onto my breasts, kissing, licking, and biting all over them—except my nipples. I whimper, writhing under his lips.

How can he do this to me? How can I be ready to rip his face off one second, and then ready to surrender myself to him completely the next?

Finally, when my body is ready to explode from the tension, I feel his teeth scraping against my nipple.

"Alexander," I moan, my back arching.

His hold on my wrists tightens as he sucks, his tongue brushing over my nipple again and again.

When he pulls back, he examines my face with a satisfied smirk. "You don't sound resigned to me."

Before I can respond, he moves on to my other breast. I moan as he rolls my nipple between his fingers before licking.

He's right—I don't sound resigned. I sound desperate.

As his mouth ruins me, his spare hand undoes my pants. He slides a hand down my front, teasing me through my underwear. His fingers find my clit and pinch through the fabric.

"Fuck, Alexander." My eyes slide closed as he bites at my nipple, quickly soothing the pain with a kiss.

"You think I want to control you?" he murmurs, biting me again. Then he pulls away, rubbing circles over the fabric between him and my clit. *"You want to be controlled.* You're fucking soaked."

My hips grind against his fingers as my mouth opens but no sounds come out.

He's right. My heart is beating so hard I think it might fly out of my chest. I may hate myself for it, but I've never felt more free than when Alexander is taking over my body.

He releases my wrists, and I immediately grip his shoulders.

He shoves my panties to the side, his fingers slipping into my folds. My groan causes him to pull back and watch as he undoes me. His eyes are on fire with lust.

He rubs small, consistent circles on my clit, his other hand closing over my throat. I lose myself in his touch, his finger sending waves of pleasure through me.

I forget that I'm in a car, topless, letting the man I'm afraid will break my heart again finger-fuck me. I forget about my anger, about him forcing me to give him another chance.

I forget everything except him. His scent of light citrus and bergamot. His mouth branding me as he sucks a bruising line in between my breasts. His finger against my clit, pushing me closer and closer to the edge.

When I'm about to come, my nails dig into his arms. "Xander, I—"

He pulls his fingers away, sitting back in his seat.

I gasp at the loss of his touch. I was *so* close. And I find myself begging before I can stop myself. "Please don't stop, please, *please.* I was almost there."

His gaze pierces me, mixed with amusement and passion. "Pack a bag, and I'll fuck you senseless all weekend."

I watch as he slowly licks his fingers clean of me. My body is settling back down, but it still aches for him.

Once he's finished, he raises an eyebrow, as if to ask, *Are you really going to challenge me right now?*

"Just give me a few minutes," I say breathlessly. Then I yank my clothes back on and stumble out of the car.

Fuck me senseless?

I already am.

. . .

By the time we make it to Alexander's house, my body has calmed down, and I'm wary of his touch. I keep my distance as he carries my bag up a flight of stairs and down a hall to his bedroom.

Something about the layout of his house is oddly familiar, but I can't quite put my finger on it. So I shrug it off as we step into a massive master bedroom.

Dark emerald curtains frame the tall windows overlooking the forest. There's a balcony to one side, overlooking the yard.

The bed is enormous, covered in a black comforter.

I let out a breath as I turn, taking it all in. Everything is perfect, not a single thing out of place.

When Alexander comes into my view, I freeze. He's watching me, a hint of satisfaction on his face, mixed with something I can't quite figure out. Want? Need? Longing? Lov—

No. No, absolutely not. There's nothing soft or loving about the man standing in front of me.

"What?" My voice comes out unsure, a little unsteady.

But he ignores me, setting my bag on the bed. "Are you hungry?"

I give him a little nod, and he grabs his phone, typing for a second before slipping it back in his pocket. Then he looks at me with that same expression.

"*What*, Alexander?"

"You don't—" He cuts himself off, shaking his head. "I have a meeting at five, unfortunately. I'll be taking it in my home office." He steps closer, snaking an arm around my waist. "I have to head back into the city for some meetings tomorrow morning as well. I'll be back before lunch."

I ignore the twinge of disappointment. Some space will be good. And it'll give me some time to write.

"But don't you worry. I have plenty of time in between to keep up my promises." He smirks, his hand sliding down my back to squeeze my ass.

"I'd really like to shower," I mumble. I already felt gross from work, but then Alexander got me turned on and sweaty.

"The bathroom is over there." He juts his chin out to the back corner of the room, where a door sits halfway open. He nibbles on my ear. "Feel free to use my shampoo. I'd love to smell myself on you."

My heart skips a beat, and before I give into him again, I pull away. "Thanks."

The bathroom is large as well, featuring a shower, but also a big tub in front of an even bigger window.

Smiling, I take in the view. When we were younger, Alexander and I loved coming up with house plans. He always made sure that the master bathroom had a large tub with a view. Now I understand why, and I make a mental note to find some wine and spend some time soaking in there while Alexander is in one of his meetings.

I shower quickly, inhaling deeply as I use Alexander's shampoo and soap. It smells good, but it's missing *him*.

When I open the frosted glass door, I find him waiting there with a plush white towel. I grab it quickly, muttering a thank you as I cover myself. Alexander has seen me naked, but that doesn't mean I enjoy being vulnerable around him.

"We have some time before dinner will be ready." He leans against the wall, his eyes soaking me in.

That's when I realize that if I want to dry myself off anytime soon, I'm going to have to get comfortable with his gaze on me. He just loves making me squirm, doesn't he?

"In the meantime, you're going to pay for that little stunt you tried to pull earlier." His voice is low, menacing.

Rolling my eyes, I start squeezing my dripping blonde hair with the towel. "Little stunt? You mean me being perfectly reasonable."

He steps forward, yanking the towel from me and tossing it onto the ground. "Reasonable? There's nothing *reasonable* about us, Sophia. You're mine, whether you want to be or not. Fuck reason."

I think it's safe to say my words got under his skin.

I reach for the towel, but he grabs me.

"Get on your knees," he growls.

I glare up at him, cursing the fact that he's a head taller than I am. There's no way I'm going to win this, so I sink down. My gaze rests on the bulge in his pants.

"The words spewing out of your mouth earlier were ridiculous, little bird, and I won't tolerate it again." His hands are busy undoing his pants. "Sounds like I'm going to have to fuck some sense *into* you before I can fuck it out of you."

My mouth waters as he pulls out his cock, already hard.

"Every time you try to *reason* with me, you can expect me to fuck that pretty little mouth of yours until the only thing leaving it is my cum. Understood?"

I nod, probably too eagerly, licking my lips.

"Then get to work."

I do, licking his shaft until the whole thing is coated in my saliva. Then I take his tip into my mouth, teasing his crown with my tongue before sucking.

"Up and down, Sophia, unless you want me to take over."

Something between a squeak and a moan sounds from the back of my throat. I do as he says, using my tongue to apply pressure as I bob my head up and down, sucking.

My jaw gets sore fast, but I keep going. If I stop, I know what'll happen, and I'm quite enjoying taking this at my own pace.

Alexander swears, one of his hands grabbing at my still-dripping hair. He doesn't try to guide me, and when I look up, I see that his eyes are closed, his face slack.

I moan as I take him in as far as I can, doing my best to suppress the gag that tries to take over. I love seeing him like this. His guard is completely down.

As if he can sense me watching him, his eyes open, and he smirks. "My turn."

His grip on my hair tightens, and he thrusts deep inside of me while holding my head still. I grab onto his thighs to keep my balance as he thrusts again, and again, claiming my mouth like it's always been his.

Something drips from in between my thighs, landing on my feet, and it's not water. *Fuck.* I hate how much I love it when he takes over me.

Tears pool in my eyes as he hits the back of my throat repeatedly, and I can feel a mix of drool and precum leaking out of my mouth. The moans from my throat are involuntary, a mix of pleasure and discomfort.

He's staring down at me with a steely resolve that should probably scare me. "You can't tell me you don't want this. It's written all over your face. I bet it's leaking from in between your legs. You want me, Sophia."

I whimper as his pace quickens. Tears stream down my face as he hits the back of my throat again and again.

He's right. He's right and I hate him for it.

I *do* want him. I'm terrified of him breaking my heart, but that doesn't mean it doesn't ache for him. Want him. Need him.

He comes with a grunt, his cum filling my mouth until it's leaking down my chin. When he's finished, he pulls out slowly, still holding my hair. "Swallow. And then clean up the mess you've made."

I do, licking him clean and wiping at my mouth. He helps me stand up, drying me with the towel he ripped off of me mere minutes before.

"Now, spread your legs and let me feel how soaked you are for me." He doesn't even give me a chance to obey, slapping my inner thighs apart.

I gasp at the feeling of his fingers slipping through my folds. He thrusts two fingers into me, and my eyes roll back into my head.

"Just as I thought." He bites my neck softly. "Unfortunately, dinner will be here momentarily. Be good, and maybe I'll eat you for dessert."

The sound that leaves my mouth is unlike anything I've ever heard before. Desperate, raw. Needy. My core aches at the loss of him.

Alexander's eyes follow my movements as he licks his fingers. I wrap the towel tightly around myself, walking on wobbly knees back into the bedroom. Clothes. I need clothes. Some type of barrier between the two of us.

There's a knock on the door, and Alexander brushes past me. I grab my bag and scamper back into the bathroom before someone sees me shivering in a towel.

Quickly, I throw on clothes, well aware that they probably won't be on me for much longer. I try to brush out my tangled hair. Anything to try to soften the crazed look in my eyes.

God, how does he pull me apart like this? Aren't I supposed to be angry at him?

But as I move back into the bedroom, there's no anger, just want.

A tray holding two plates sits on the bed, along with Alexander. He's sipping a glass of wine, leaning back on one hand, gazing at me.

He has that look on his face again. The one I can't quite figure out.

"Stop looking at me like that." I throw my bag onto the floor and climb up onto the bed.

"Then stop making me want to fuck you on every surface in this house." His stare glides over my legs, to my shorts and tank top. "I told you that first night, Sophia. I want to see you in my house. Clothed. Naked. In nothing but heels. I want to watch you fuck yourself and come from every angle, and then take you as mine until you can't walk. In every room. On every surface. Every day."

I can feel my cheeks heating. Looking down, I grab my own glass of wine and take a sip. He already has my body wound up and begging for him. Why does he insist on torturing me more?

"You'd better hurry up if you want a piece of me. Don't forget about my meeting."

I straighten, glancing at the clock on his bedside table. It's almost four. With a bashful glance at Alexander, I grab my fork and start shoving food into my mouth.

Flavor explodes on my tongue. The dish looks like simple pasta, but it tastes amazing. Garlic and herbs dance in my mouth, and I let out a moan.

Alexander grins, and the sight of pure happiness on his face shocks me. "Anna is a ridiculously good cook."

I nod in agreement, taking another bite and savoring the delicious cheese sauce. Alexander continues watching me, and I do my best not to squirm.

When I finish, he reaches out, wiping away sauce from my bottom lip with his thumb. Then, silently, he picks up the tray and carries it to the dresser.

My heart picks up its pace. But he doesn't turn to me. Instead, he disappears through a door—presumably to his closet.

He comes out holding a dark blue off-the-shoulder gown. Fabric spills from his arms, silver embroidery on the skirt glistening in the light.

"We should make sure this fits you."

I let out a short breath of disappointment, but strip quickly. He helps me get the dress on, zipping it up—but not before leaving a trail of kisses up my spine.

He stops partway up, pushing the dress out of the way. His fingers brush against the right side of my back, and then his lips press to the spot of my tattoo.

Little bird.

I stare at my reflection in the full-length mirror he leads me to. Even with no makeup and still-tangled hair, I look like a princess.

My shoulders look sexy as hell, and so does my collarbone. A small necklace would look perfect dangling from my neck.

Alexander's hands slip over the shiny fabric hugging my waist before flaring out at my hips. I turn to face him, the layers of fabric swishing against the floor.

"Just a little long," I say. "Nothing a pair of heels won't fix."

Heat flashes through Alexander's eyes. "As long as you don't expect to take them off when we get home."

I smile as he steps back, taking me in.

After a few seconds, he says, "You're going to hate me for this."

My smile fades. "What?"

But he stays silent, unzipping my dress and helping me step out of it. He disappears back into the closet, coming out to find me still standing there, naked except for my panties.

"I'll hate you for what, Alexander?"

He still doesn't answer. Just kisses me, lifting me into his arms. My legs lock around his waist.

When he sets me on the edge of the bed, it's with such gentleness that I look at him with confusion. But he slips my underwear off, spreading my legs. We both moan as his finger finds my clit, coated in my arousal.

"Why would I hate you for this?" My voice is breathy, light.

A flash of Alexander's usual arrogance graces his face, but he shakes his head. "Just relax. Forget about everything except me."

Before I can protest, he kisses me, wrapping his free arm around my waist. He tastes like wine and smells of citrus and bergamot and him.

His lips leave mine, just for them to kiss my breasts. His tongue flicks out over one of my nipples.

Closing my eyes, I do as he says. Every thought except him leaves my mind. All I know is his touch, his breath, his scent.

My head hits the soft mattress as he pushes me onto my back. He kneels, tugging me until I'm almost falling off of the bed.

When his tongue circles my clit, I grip at the comforter, doing my best not to squirm. His hands are holding my hips, his tongue and lips working in perfect harmony to unravel me completely.

When he thrusts two of his fingers inside of me, curling them in just the right way, I can't help the loud moan that comes out.

He continues just like that, his other hand holding my hips still as I try to grind against his mouth.

"Alexander," I gasp when he quickens the pace of his fingers.

He lets out a deep chuckle as he scrapes his teeth against my clit. Then he sucks it into his mouth.

"Fuck," I whisper, my legs shaking as he returns to what he was doing.

I'm close. He knows I'm close. At this point, anything will push me over the edge.

His fingers brush my peaked nipples, adding the perfect amount of extra sensation. My back arches, a cry escaping my lips, and then—

A loss of all sensation.

"No," I plead. "Keep going. Xander, I was so close."

He's standing, his gaze on his glistening fingers. "Told you you'd hate me."

"Alexander," I yell, pushing myself up onto my elbows. My body is shaking with need. *Please.*"

"I have to get to my meeting, little bird." He leans forward, his fingers prodding my lips open until I suck myself off of him.

I moan at my own taste, knowing this is what he was delving into mere seconds ago. Before I let his fingers go, I clamp down with my teeth. Not hard enough to draw blood, but enough that it'll still hurt.

He doesn't wince—just gives me an evil smile. "Don't ever say shit like you said earlier, and this won't happen again."

I release his fingers and grab onto his shirt. "Fuck you."

He chuckles, taking my hands in his. He nibbles at the inside of my wrists, licking and kissing away the pain as I stare up at him. Then he pushes me back onto bed, falling with me, pinning my arms above my head.

"Xander!" I say, still frustrated, but my legs part for him instead of kneeing him in the balls.

"Don't you *dare* think about finishing yourself off." His breath is hot on my face. "When I come back, you'd better be ready for me to fuck you to oblivion. Your orgasms are mine, and I want to see your face when you scream my name."

I give him a wide-eyed nod, cursing the ache between my legs.

He begins to straighten, but then that devilish look fills his face. He leans forward again, keeping my arms above my head, and sucks a nipple into his mouth.

The sound that leaves my mouth is half-sob, half moan, and 100% desperation. I arch my back to meet his mouth, swearing as he flicks his tongue out.

When he moves to my other breast, my hips are grinding against air, and I can't help the pleading words leaving my mouth.

And then he's gone, with a simple goodbye and a light kiss on my nose.

I don't know how long I lay there, panting, resisting the urge to let my fingers slip inside of me.

Eventually, I get up and pull my clothes back on. While I want to lie on the bed fuming about the fact that Alexander denied me an orgasm *again,* this is precious time to get some work done.

So I grab my laptop and start writing, doing my best to ignore my wanting body.

CHAPTER 5

Sophia

"Did you miss me?" Alexander shuts the door behind him quietly, already tugging off his tie.

I glare at him. "Not one bit."

"Good. Then you won't mind if I shower." He disappears into the closet again, coming back out wearing nothing but his boxers.

"Do whatever you want," I say, managing to keep my voice even. My eyes, however, stay glued to his perfectly-chiseled abs.

Goddammit. I want him, I need him. But the past few hours without his touch has helped me come back to my senses a bit.

I want *out* of this situation, this screwed-up version of a relationship. Not deeper into it. And if I can't control myself whenever he's around, I'm fucked.

So I go back to typing away, ignoring him when he breezes past to the bathroom. I can practically feel the irritation rolling off of him.

I expect to hear the shower turn on, but when I don't, I turn around to find him reading over my shoulder. "Alexander!"

He smirks. "What're you working on? Looks good."

"None of your goddamned business, Xander. It's private." I shut my laptop. How did I not hear him sneak up behind me?

"A book, huh?"

My cheeks are burning. "Go take your stupid shower."

"Is that what you want?" He crawls onto the bed, grabbing my waist and pulling me onto his lap. His hand cups my breast. "Is that truly, *truly* what you want?"

I stare up into his brown, gold-flecked eyes, taking a deep breath to calm my racing heart. His pupils are dilated, lust etched into every detail of his beautiful face.

But there's something else there, too. Passion. A passion that runs so deep it feels endless.

He wants you. Forever. He's not going to leave again. He never wanted to in the first place.

The thought sends hope soaring through me, but I shut it down. How can that be true? How can he say that he never wanted to leave me when he disappeared from my life for five years?

Alexander has always had a dark side. And while I was subject to his bullying for a short while in high school, he didn't date me to toy with me. He dated me because he wanted me, forever. I *know* that.

Now? Now I'm not sure. What if he's turned back to his old ways? What if I'm just a toy to him? Something to play with until he feels like breaking me and watching me bleed.

"Soph?" Alexander's voice pulls me out of my thoughts. There's a touch of concern in his eyes. His arms tighten around me protectively.

"I don't know what I want," I mumble. I focus on his chest, not wanting to see the disappointment on his face.

How am I supposed to know if he's telling the truth? If he means it when he says he doesn't want to lose me again. What if this is all some elaborate prank to him? Something to entertain him. Or worse, what if he does mean it?

What if he means it, but when things get hard again, he doesn't choose me? He just *thinks* he will.

I blink back tears. This isn't the time to cry. Alexander is half-naked, we're sitting on his bed, and I can feel his boner.

I expect him to make up my mind for me. To kiss me, manipulate me, bend my will until it's the same as his.

But he doesn't.

He just sits there, rubbing my back, holding me close.

My shock brings a lump to my throat, but I swallow it down. Just because he knows how to make me feel safe doesn't mean I *am* safe.

I can't let this mean anything.

He kisses the top of my head, cradling it with one of his hands and bringing it to rest on his chest. His heartbeat is steady. Strong.

Fear shoots through me at the compassionate gesture. But there's hope, too, and this time, I let it take over.

We stay there, his fingers tracing circles on my back, and I curl into the heat of his body. When my eyes droop and my body relaxes, he rocks me back and forth gently.

At some point, I have some vague moment of embarrassment, realizing I'm falling asleep before the sun has even set. But it's overtaken by my inability to keep my eyes open.

When Alexander moves me under the covers, I barely open my eyes enough to watch him take my laptop and set it on his dresser. Then he leans over me, kissing my forehead, before mumbling something into my hair.

Something that sounds familiar. Warm.

But my mind is already drifting, and I don't catch his words before sleep overtakes me.

. . .

I wake up in a cocoon of warmth. Sun is streaming through the windows, and a heavy hand rests on my hip.

I can't help the smile that creeps onto my face. I love sleeping in, and waking up in such a luxurious bed, with a mountain of pillows? Heaven.

And the man next to me?

Rolling over, I take in Alexander's sleeping form. He looks so peaceful, so calm. All of the tension that's usually in his jaw is missing, and his hair is a mess, falling onto his forehead in dark locks.

I could get used to this.

The thought enters my mind before I can put up a guard around my heart. I squeeze my eyes shut against the pain.

"Good morning, beautiful," Alexander says in a deep, half-asleep voice. His hand snakes around my waist and pulls me closer to him.

I snuggle up to him, pressing a kiss to his chest. "Hi."

He looks down at me, relaxed. Happy. Almost . . . relieved?

"I'll never get enough of seeing you in my bed, Sophia."

Smiling, I kiss him lightly. But I don't reply. What am I supposed to say? That I'd love to wake up with him every morning? That I'm afraid he's going to break my heart? That I want him but hate him at the same time?

He doesn't seem to need an answer, though. He just holds me, running one hand through my hair. His eyes close again, a faint smile on his lips.

"When are your meetings?" I mumble, just as there's a knock on the door. I jump, but he holds onto me.

Glancing at the clock, he says, "I have time," before sliding out of bed. He grabs a bathrobe and ties it tightly before answering the door.

An older woman pushes past him with a cart full of food, grinning at him and stopping short when she spots me. Anna.

"My, my," she says, her eyes twinkling. "I was beginning to think the two of you would never get back together."

"Good morning, Anna," I say with a smile. It warms my heart that she recognizes me. But I guess I saw her nearly every day when Alexander and I were dating.

"Alexander, I love you dearly. You know that. But if you break her heart again, I'll see to it personally that all of your meals are under-seasoned and bland." Then Anna turns to me. "Darling, I'm so glad to see you. I won't bug you now, but I'd love for you to stop by the kitchen sometime so we can catch up."

"Will do." My heart squeezes, and I wrap one of the blankets around me. Without Alexander here, it's cold.

"All right, you two enjoy. Just text me if you need anything, Alexander." With that, she leaves, closing the door behind her.

Alexander wheels the cart to the bed. There are two plates with pancakes stacked high, little bowls with berries, and two mugs of steaming coffee. He hands me the one with cream, taking the black one for himself.

"Is there sugar in this?" I say, letting the coffee warm my hands.

He nods. "I told her how you like it."

Fucking hell. He's not making it easy to keep my emotional distance.

"Thank you," I murmur, sipping on my coffee. It's perfect.

We eat in silence, sitting on the edge of bed. The food is delicious, reminding me of the breakfasts Anna would make Alexander and I after we'd meet up for our early Saturday morning runs.

Smiling, I think about how he always made sure I drank enough water and always slowed down when I couldn't keep up with him.

He was stoic and unreadable to everyone else. But when he was with me, he treated me like I was the most precious thing on earth.

"What are you thinking about?" Alexander says with a mouthful of berries.

"Oh—uh, just how I fell asleep so early. Sorry."

"You needed it." He brushes some hair behind my shoulders. "You have nothing to apologize for."

I stare at him for a second too long before turning back to my food. This isn't the man who invaded my life and won't let me go. This is the boy who was willing to do anything to make me happy.

That boy deserves a fair chance.

Biting my lip, I risk a glance at Alexander, only to find him watching me. That mysterious look is back on his face again.

"Either stop looking at me like that, or tell me what you're thinking." My voice comes out softer than I meant.

He looks away, and I feel a twinge of disappointment. Because I know what I *want* that look to mean, and while I want it, it scares the hell out of me.

We finish breakfast, and Alexander has to leave pretty quickly. My heart doesn't want him to go, but my mind is happy for the space.

He kisses me goodbye, clutching at my waist, and when he pulls away, I can see pain in his eyes. He doesn't want to hold back. Honestly, I'm confused why he is. It goes against everything he's done over the past week or so.

Once he's gone, I get to work, cuddling under the blankets with my laptop. It doesn't take me long to get into a groove, and soon Alexander is the last thing on my mind. He texts me sometime around eleven, letting me know that his meetings are running late, and that he won't be back until later in the afternoon.

Most of me is relieved. It gives me more time to work, and I really can't afford to put off writing today.

But a small part of me misses Alexander. Which sends me tumbling into a confusing swirl of thoughts.

Do I want him? Do I trust him?

Does he want me? And if so, just as a fling, or for forever?

What if he wants forever? *Really* wants it?

Is that what I want?

Underneath all my worry and fear, I think I do. But is that just because he's good in bed? Because he held me while I fell asleep last night?

The part of me that's still hurting and holding onto my last little bit of common sense says, *He didn't even give you a choice in coming here this weekend. Or in giving him a second chance.*

But the other part of me? *He said he doesn't want to lose you again. And what about the way he looked at you this morning? He smiled. He held you. He kissed you with so much passion.*

I don't know what to think. I don't know what to do. It's like I'm being torn in two, and I don't even have a say in how it happens.

Frustrated and exhausted, I dive back into my work for hours. Because no matter how much I need to figure out my shit with Xander, I *can't* get behind on this book.

Chapter 6

Sophia

My chest feels tight as we pull up to a familiar-looking mansion. "Vanessa? This is at Vanessa's house?"

"Her parents' home, yes."

"You could've at least warned me," I grumble, shooting him a glare across the back seat.

Alexander just shrugs, nodding to the driver as he slows to a stop by the front steps. "You'll be fine, Soph."

I roll my eyes as he gets out and walks around the car to get my door.

Vanessa Ellison was my worst enemy in high school. Not only did she constantly try to separate me from Alexander, but she had to make every aspect of my life hell. Our families were direct competitors with each other in most things: business, who got the spotlight, who had the more successful kid, etc. It was a constant battle for who could be more picture-perfect. And the family feud bled into my relationship with Vanessa.

When she won, she never let me hear the end of it. And she also couldn't wait to get her hands on Alexander the second we were broken up.

He didn't even try to stop her.

Jealousy flares in my stomach, and I accept Alexander's hand stiffly when he helps me out of the car.

Before he even closes the door, he presses me into his body. My breath escapes me at the feeling of his hard muscles against my stomach.

"She'll be here," he says. "And I don't give a single fuck. There isn't room in my heart for anyone but you, Sophia. And if Vanessa doesn't already know that, it'll become clear tonight."

"What do you mean she doesn't already know?" I hate the vicious undertone of my voice.

Alexander hesitates, letting out a sigh. "What can I say? She's relentless."

Taking a deep breath, I pull away from Alexander, but my actions are in vain. Regardless of what's happened—or hasn't happened—between the two of them, now isn't the time to show that I'm unhappy.

I have no desire to be paraded around in front of a whole bunch of people who witnessed my family's fall from grace years ago. But I'll be damned if it looks like Alexander and I are together but having problems, as well.

I don't know what's going to happen between Alexander and me. But the thought of seeing the look of quiet shock on Vanessa's face when she realizes that he's mine and *only* mine?

Yeah, I want to see that.

So I let Alexander kiss me lightly before taking his arm and heading up the stairs to the tall front doors.

When he finally made it home earlier today, he'd been exhausted and grumpy. Spending the day in the office wasn't what he wanted for today. I may have been relieved at the time to write, sure. But seeing Alexander walk into his room full of tension and stress was heartbreaking.

I'm sure he's been under a lot of pressure since his father's death.

I squeeze his arm as we enter the Ellison mansion, following a staff member as he leads us to the ballroom. I can already hear the classical music drifting through the halls, and the thought of maybe getting to dance with Alexander makes my heart skip a beat.

The room is well-lit with glistening chandeliers and tall candles at every table. The middle of the room is empty, and a few couples are dancing, slowly swaying to the music. A wave of relief hits me as I see the amount of people I don't recognize.

"Alexander!" A woman in a hot pink dress waddles over to us. Upon closer inspection, I realize with dread who she is.

"Good evening, mother." Alexander kisses her on the cheek, and I can't help but notice the stiffness in his movements.

"I was wondering when you were going to show up. And who's this?" Everly glances at me with a smile, only for it to fall. "What are you doing with *her?*"

"Nice to see you too, Everly." I plaster on my best fake smile.

"Alexander, you can do better than—than *that*," Everly hisses, glancing around. "What about Vanessa?"

"My love life isn't any of your business." Alexander loops his arm around my waist.

"My dear, you know you need to make a better decision than this. What will people think? And you know you need to secure the future of your father's business. What better way to do that than marria-"

"*My* business is secure, mother," Alexander spits out, loud enough to make Everly glance around with concern. "And I don't need a marriage to keep it that way. Worry about yourself for once."

Alexander turns, dragging me with him as he heads to the opposite side of the room. A group of three men in perfectly-tailored suits stand in a tight-knit circle. One of them glances up, and I'm met with a pair of familiar blue eyes.

Blaze Grayson. I'll never forget the kind, blond jokester who helped make high school less miserable.

"Aha!" he exclaims, waving his arms and almost spilling the glass of champagne in his hand. "Is this why you've been so secretive lately, Alex? Welcome back, Soph."

I grin, embracing Blaze as he shoves past the other two and envelopes me in a hug. I can feel Alexander tensing beside me, but I don't care.

"Took you two long enough." Dominic winks at me. While he shares the same blue eyes as his younger brother, Dominic is a tad taller than Blaze, and with dark brown hair instead of blond.

Once Blaze has finished hugging me, Dominic gives me a nod—probably because of the murderous glare Alexander is giving him.

"I didn't miss you one bit." The other man grins at me. Hair the same color as Dominic's, flopping onto his forehead in loose ringlets.

"You look familiar." I narrow my eyes, looking him over. He shares some of the same facial features as the Grayson brothers, but his eyes are gray.

"We met a few times when you were in high school. I'm these idiots' cousin." He jerks his head toward Blaze and Dominic. "I heard quite a few stories about the four of you back in the day."

Blushing, I take Alexander's arm again. The four of us were quite the friend group. One girl, three guys, but I never felt unsafe. They'd grown up in the same neighborhood as Alexander, so we spent a lot of time together after school and in the summers.

We had a blast together—until everything fell apart.

"Felix works with us now," Dominic says, clapping him on the back. "He's great with computers and that shit, which is great to have."

"Right." I smile politely, racking my brain and trying to remember what the Grayson's business is.

"Private security," Blaze says with a grin.

"Thanks. Sorry, I should've remembered."

He shrugs it off. "No biggie. Tell me, how have things been with you? What've you been up to?"

My heart all but stops. This is exactly what I was afraid of, yet I still haven't figured out a good way to say that I've been struggling in every aspect of my life. "Not much." My grip on Alexander's arm tightens.

"The important thing is that she's here with us. With me." Alexander drops a light kiss on my head. "Now, where'd you get that champagne?"

"Oh, this?" Blaze lifts up his flute. "This is fake stuff. Tastes like ass. We're working tonight. Undercover." He winks at me.

"The Ellisons insisted." Dominic rolls his eyes. "Never mind that we have plenty of other guys who could've handled this job without us."

"That's what you get for being the best of the best." Alexander smirks before murmuring in my ear, "I'm going to get us something to drink. Are you comfortable with the guys, or do you want to come with me?"

I gulp. I *want* to stay glued to Alexander's side all night. But I also don't want to look like a lost puppy dog following him around. "I'll stay." With the best smile of confidence I can muster, I let him go.

"Soooo." Blaze sidles up to me, slipping a big arm around my shoulders. He was never skinny, but he's bulked up a lot since I last saw him. "You and Hendricks, huh? Wanna tell me how he managed to win you back?"

I bite back my response of, *He hasn't.* "A lot of luck, I guess. Just watch out, he's as possessive as ever."

Felix barks out a laugh. "Possessive? Alexander? I've only ever seen him treat his women with cold indifference."

"Not Soph." Dominic's quiet seriousness cuts through our laughter, and I meet his gaze.

However much I hate that Alexander has had *other women,* it makes my heart swell with happiness that he treats me differently. Maybe he really does mean what he's been saying.

That thought is shattered in an instant, though, as another one replaces it:

Or maybe he just wants to make sure you don't get away until he's finished breaking you into pieces again.

I shiver, and Blaze tightens his arm around me. "You always did get cold easily. Want my jacket?" His grin is mischievous as he starts slipping off his jacket.

"No, I'm actually not cold. I was just . . . thinking, I guess." Before they ask any more questions, I turn the conversation back around. "So how long have you guys been at Grayson Security?"

Dominic nods. "I worked through all of college, and Blaze through his last three years. Dad retired, so I run everything now. Couldn't do it without these two."

I smile. It's a relief to know that Dominic and Blaze are still close. They were inseparable in high school. We all were.

"That fucking *bitch.*"

I feel Blaze's whole body tense, and when I follow his gaze, mine does too.

Alexander has been stopped by his mother, and a gorgeous brunette in a fuchsia gown has an arm wrapped tightly around his waist.

Vanessa.

"Some things never change." I ignore the bitterness in my voice. Who the hell does she think she is?

I almost storm over there and rip her off of him by her hair, but I stop myself. Because, when it comes down to it, Alexander isn't *actually* mine. And I'm still not sure if I trust him.

And as I watch him give her a heart-stopping smile, the little bit of trust he *does* have begins to slip away.

"I'll handle this," Dominic growls, separating from the group and making a beeline for Everly's dream couple.

Blaze turns me away, leading me to the dance floor. "Let's make him jealous, shall we?"

"Are you sure you want to experience Alexander's wrath?" I say with a giggle. But I don't hesitate when Blaze pulls me into his arms, waltzing me around the room.

"The bastard needs to know what a treasure he has. God, I wanna kill him sometimes."

I bite back the urge to ask him if he thinks Alexander's feelings for me are genuine. But thankfully, I keep my mouth shut. How would he know?

"I feel like we're in high school again." I let out a sigh, trying to get a peek at Alexander, but Blaze keeps me angled so I can't see.

But then he stops as a dark figure stumbles into us, spilling wine all over Blaze's crisp white shirt.

"Oh, fuck! I'm so sorry!"

I tense at that voice. Tristan.

Jesus Christ, I really *am* back in high school.

"What the hell, man?" Blaze steps back, holding me at arm's length so he doesn't stain my dress.

Tristan's eyes flash. "Really, it was an accident. I just wasn't paying attention." He turns toward me. "Surprised to see you here. Alexander hasn't finished his fun with you yet?"

"Fuck off, Goodwin." Any trace of humor has disappeared from Blaze's face, and his tone is as sharp as a razor.

"Or what?" Tristan looks him up and down. "Besides, you need to get yourself cleaned up. Shall we finish the dance, Sophia?"

I don't give him the satisfaction of a reply. Instead, I scan the room for Alexander and Dominic. They aren't where they were a few minutes ago. Turning, I catch them disappearing down a hallway.

What the actual hell.

Tristan and Blaze are having a standoff of sorts, both glaring and throwing insults at each other. So I slip away, quietly exiting the ballroom.

Muffled voices come from behind a half-open door, and just as I'm about to burst in, I stop at the anger in Dominic's tone.

"You're being an idiot, Alex. Dragging her into this? She deserves better."

"I've got it under control."

"Under control?" Dominic practically shouts. "Vanessa might be a menace, but Tristan? He's out for blood. You should've waited until you had your shit together before going after her."

Alexander says something I don't quite make out, and Dominic snorts in response.

"She was safe, living her own little life. But now? Alex, you know how far Tristan has gone in the past. You're fucking around with her *life*. He'll do anything to get to you."

My hand falls away from the door. Whose life? Mine? What the hell is going on?

There's silence for a few seconds, and I can imagine the two men glaring at each other. Then Dominic says, "Look, at least tell Vanessa to fuck off. You broke Sophia's heart once, and if you do it again, I'll beat you to a bloody pulp."

I shiver. There's absolutely no indication in Dominic's voice that he's joking. Just anger—a *lot* of anger.

"You know I can't. She's close to Tristan, and we might need her."

"Then figure something out, Alex!"

"I'm not losing Soph again, Dominic. I love her."

"Then start acting like it, you fuckwit." There's a dull hitting noise, and I can only imagine that Alexander just got slapped on the back of the head. "Take care of Vanessa before she tries anything stupid."

I lean against the wall, taking shallow breaths.

Did I hear Alexander correctly?

He loves me.

I shake my head. No. No, that's not possible. We've barely seen each other in years. Maybe he's obsessed, but love? *Love?*

The two men continue arguing, but I barely register their voices. My mind is reeling, going back and forth between *Alexander loves me* and *Why the fuck is my life in danger?*

After a few more minutes of Alexander and Dominic's harsh voices lashing out at each other, I realize I need to get out of here before I get caught. I have a feeling this isn't a conversation I'm meant to hear.

With quiet steps, I head back into the ballroom and snag a flute of champagne off a tray from a passing server. *Finally.* Hopefully some alcohol will help me deal with the disaster that tonight is becoming.

I do my best to stay out of sight, looking for Blaze—hell, I'd even go for Felix right now.

Unfortunately, Everly finds me first. She wraps a hand around my arm, and while her grip is weak, her nails dig into my skin.

"Stay away from my son," she hisses. She reeks of an overbearing floral perfume. "He deserves better than you do. You're just getting in the way."

I yank my arm away from her, noting the scrapes from her fingernails. "Listen, Everly. Your son is an adult. So why don't you start treating him like one?"

The two of us have never gotten along, but I've never been so frank with her before. I was too young, too afraid of her. So the shock on her face doesn't surprise me. When she stumbles back, I smirk and walk away.

"God, there you are!" Felix appears out of thin air, falling into step beside me. "I lost you while Blaze and Tristan were hogging the dance floor. Damn, talk about sexual tension."

I can't help it. I let out a laugh, almost snorting a sip of champagne out of my nose. When I spot Dominic and Alexander walking toward us, I straighten up, waving at the two of them. Dominic still looks pissed, but Alexander is as put-together and calm as ever.

"Sorry about that." He kisses my head, planting his hand firmly on my lower back. "Where's Blaze?"

I open my mouth to explain, but Felix cuts me off with a look. "He spilled his drink all over him, the clumsy oaf. He'll be back soon."

I smile, keeping my mouth shut. Maybe it's for the best that Alexander doesn't know Tristan tried to get his hands on me again.

Thankfully, the rest of the evening flows by smoothly. We chat with the guys for a while before Alexander and I break off from the group. He introduces me to a couple people, making small talk with some other men I'm sure he's trying to strengthen relationships with.

A couple of times, I catch Tristan staring at me. It sends shivers down my spine. Blaze eventually drapes his jacket over my shoulders, but when Alexander notices, he yanks it off of me and gives me his.

It might sound silly, but it makes me smile. I inhale Alexander's scent of bergamot and citrus for the rest of the night, staying close to him. And to my delight, his hands rarely leave me.

When he catches me yawning behind my hand, he plants a kiss on the top of my head. "Are you ready to head out?"

"If you don't mind."

It's been nice to catch up with the guys, but I'm tired. And I can practically feel Tristan's stare on me wherever I go. So when we start our goodbyes, relief floods me. By the time we're sitting in the backseat of the car, I'm ready to curl up on Alexander's lap and fall asleep.

Before I've even settled, he pulls me onto the middle seat. "I want you close to me," he murmurs in my ear, reaching over and buckling me in.

I smile, pressing my lips to his. His hand cups my face.

In this moment, it really does feel like Alexander loves me. And when he deepens our kiss, his tongue running across my bottom lip, I want his words to be true.

But then an image of Vanessa standing with her arm around him flashes through my mind. Tristan's words, implying that I'm just a fling, are like tiny stabs at my heart.

When I pull away, he tightens his grip around my waist. I dip my head down and rest it on his chest.

He's only possessive of me. Dominic said so. I'm special to him.

But he didn't stop Vanessa from running her hands all over him.

Besides, do I really want someone who's overly possessive?

But he said he loves me.

I close my eyes as tears start to well up. Alexander is playing with my heart enough, but apparently he's also playing with my life. What the fuck does that mean? How? What was Dominic implying when he said that Tristan might try using me to get to Alexander?

Yet again, I come back to the same place I keep finding myself.

Of course I want Alexander. He's smart. Gorgeous. And I've always felt safe around him. But can I trust him?

That's what I just can't quite figure out.

. . .

Hushed voices and sunlight wake me in the morning. I blink my eyes open, seeing Alexander at the door, pulling in a cart and talking quietly.

Breakfast in bed, again? Anna is an angel.

When he closes the door, I stretch with a yawn.

After we got home last night, Alexander ran us a bath and then gave me a back massage. He was tense the entire time, but I didn't prod him. Considering his argument with Dominic, I had a pretty good idea what was bugging him.

We fell into bed pretty quickly, too tired for more than a little kissing. Alexander held back, for what reason I'm not quite sure. Is he really giving me space? Letting me figure out what I want?

What if it turns out I don't want him?

The mattress moves again, and I realize I've closed my eyes. A hand brushes hair out of my face, and I let out a small moan.

"Good morning."

I force my eyes open, and I'm greeted with an angelic smile. The morning sun sheds bright light on Alexander's features, warming his brown eyes.

"Morning." I push myself up into a sitting position, keeping the sheet over my breasts. "What time is it?"

"A little after nine." He leaves a trail of kisses down my jaw. He smells of sweat and rain and the outdoors. "Coffee?"

I nod, brushing my hair behind my shoulders and getting a better look at him. His hair is slightly damp, along with his shorts. He's not wearing a shirt, but his shoulders and chest are shining with moisture.

"Woke up early and couldn't get back to sleep. Went on a run." He hands me my coffee, kissing my nose. "I'm gonna hop in the shower real quick. Then I'll eat with you."

I sip my coffee slowly while he showers, feeling like absolute royalty. I could get used to waking up in this beautifully dark room, in this gigantic bed, with breakfast wheeled to us every morning.

If things actually work out like that.

I shiver. Why do my thoughts always have to sabotage my happiness?

I slip out of bed and put on some panties and my hoodie. Then I grab my coffee and stand in front of the windows, gazing out into the forest.

How does Alexander ever leave with a view like this?

I stay there, watching as light rain falls and the wind blows through the trees. My coffee is delicious, and I wish I could stay here forever.

"Fucking hell, Sophia."

Turning, I find Alexander standing in the doorway of the bathroom. A towel is knotted at his waist, and his dark hair is messy and tousled.

"You know you can't do that to me." He's behind me in a second, pressing my back to his front. His fingers trace over his name, embroidered over my heart in dark thread.

"Do what?" My voice is innocent, but I watch my reflection in the window as a wry smile takes over my face.

"I've been patient, little bird. *Very* patient. I had a hard enough time last night, seeing you in my jacket. I almost pulled you into a spare room so I could take you then. You can't ask me to hold back when you wear this."

"Who said I'm asking?" I set my mug on the windowsill before turning to face him. Placing my hands on his bare chest, I rise onto my tiptoes and kiss him.

With a grunt, he picks me up. He squeezes my ass as I lock my legs around him. His scent is intoxicating—clean and citrus and him.

Alexander wastes no time, tearing my underwear off but leaving the hoodie on. Maybe it's because he knows I'm cold, or maybe it's because he likes seeing his name on me.

He kisses me until I'm breathless. My hands pull his towel away, and he groans when I wrap my fingers around his hard cock.

"Please don't stop this time," I whisper.

He kisses my neck. "I won't. I promise." He twists a hand into my hair. "I lo- I—I teased you enough yesterday."

He pulls my hand away, guiding his dick into my wet folds. It slips up, and he rubs it against my clit. He goes around in small circles before moving to an up-and-down motion, coaxing moans out of me with ease.

Finally, he stops, and his tip is replaced by his thumb. "Are you ready?" he whispers.

I nod, tangling my fingers in his hair. When he thrusts into me, it takes all my willpower not to scream.

The feeling of him inside me is overwhelming, and I can't help the noises leaving my mouth. His thumb rubs against my clit, shooting lightning bolts of pleasure through my body.

"Fuck." Alexander's voice is rough. He tightens the hand tangled in my hair.

His thrusts quicken, and it shoves me over the edge. I cry out as I grip his shoulders. Alexander comes a few seconds later, slowing until he comes to a stop.

"You're fucking amazing," he says with a shudder, his lips crashing against mine.

My heart is beating wildly. The breaths I do manage to take are hard and short. "Xander," I whisper, my arms wrapping around his neck.

"Yes?" He rests his head in the crook of my neck, and I feel his wet hair against my cheek.

"I don't want this morning to ever end." I let my eyes slide closed again as he pulls out of me.

"Neither do I." He collapses onto the bed, pulling me close. My body meets his, my soft curves molding into his hard muscle. Tightening his arms around me, he drops a kiss on the top of my head.

I lay there as my heartbeat calms and my body comes down from the high of Alexander. Soon, I can't keep my eyes closed. All I know is the softness of the sheets and the strength of Alexander's arms.

At some point, his deep, soft voice drifts through my sleepy mind.

"I love you, Sophia Aswall. And I always will."

Chapter 7

Sophia

"He told me he loves me."

Lissa stares at me, a half-finished iced latte in her hands. "He did *what?*"

"I don't think I was supposed to hear. I was falling asleep. He said he loves me, Lissa. And that he always will."

Yesterday was blissful. We stayed home, swimming, soaking in his hot tub, and rolling around in bed like teenagers who couldn't get enough of each other.

When he dropped me off at home last night, I almost asked him to spend the night with me. But thankfully, I found my sense before that. Victoria and Rachel would never let me hear the end of it.

"Sophia, that's . . . that's a lot. You guys haven't even become an official thing yet."

Sighing, I say, "I know."

I've refrained from telling Lissa about Tristan and the lecture Dominic gave Xander about messing around with my life. I wasn't sure what it all meant, and I certainly don't want to worry Lissa.

But I need a second opinion. My heart is all over the place, desperately wanting to tell Xander that I love him, too. But panic alarms are sounding in my head, screaming that this is all too fast, too movie-like.

"It's weird, right? We broke up five years ago. And it's not like we've been friends."

Lissa shakes her head, finishing the iced latte and handing it to a waiting customer. "Look, he seems great for the most part. And I don't really know him. But there are parts of his personality that are just—" She pauses, scrunching up her face.

"Dark?"

"I didn't want to say it."

Sighing, I lean against the edge of the counter. The shop has been slow today, and I'm grateful for it. "I just don't know what to do. I want to give him a second chance, but I'm scared."

"I know, babe." She grabs a cloth from a sanitizer bucket and starts wiping down the sticky counters. "You want my opinion? Don't give up on him yet. But proceed with caution, okay? I don't want to see you get hurt."

"I'm trying. He just—he puts a spell on me whenever he's around."

She smirks. "That's actually kind of cute."

The bell on the door jingles, and we both look up to see Brent walking in, his head down.

Fuck.

Over the weekend, I completely forgot about him. He was so disappointed when Alexander kissed me in front of him.

Brent orders quietly, his shoulders tense. He barely even looks at me.

Before I hand him his coffee, I hesitate. "Brent, look, I'm so-"

"Don't worry about it. I had my chance, and I lost it." He finally looks at me with a joyless smile. "I just hope he makes you happy."

With that, he takes his coffee and leaves. And I'm left standing behind the counter, my heart squeezing in pain.

I watch as Brent's figure disappears down the sidewalk.

Happy. *Happy.*

Is that how Alexander makes me feel? Is that how he *will* make me feel in the future if I stay with him?

I don't know, but I need to figure it out soon.

. . .

The next few days are uneventful. My shifts are as long and exhausting as ever, and Brent stays tense whenever he comes in. Part of me wonders why he hasn't just started going to a different coffee shop.

On Friday, Alexander picks me up for another night in his mansion before a Saturday morning brunch his mother is hosting. I'm not terribly excited about it, considering Everly's words to me last weekend. But Alexander insists.

So Saturday morning, after Alexander wakes me up with his head in between my legs, we head out.

I'm wearing a black sundress, Alexander in shorts and a polo. It's warm on the outdoor patio at the Hendricks mansion, and it takes me back to summers spent lounging by the pool with the boys.

"Oh, Alexander! I didn't realize you were bringing a date." Everly breaks off from the group of people she was chatting up. Giving me a tight smile, she embraces Alexander. "Still, I'm glad you're here. Your sister should be down soon."

"Perfect. How's she holding up?"

Everly sighs, rolling her eyes. "Ridiculously emotional. I don't understand why she isn't over that boy yet. It's been months! Maybe you can talk some sense into her."

I shoot Xander a questioning look, but he annoyingly ignores it. Instead, he continues a shallow conversation with his mother. When I spot Blaze and Dominic walking down the stairs from the house, I slip away through the crowd of pastel-clad elites.

Dominic gives me a smile and a quick kiss on the cheek. Then with a wink, he heads straight for Alexander and Everly.

"Off to the rescue." Blaze watches as his brother interrupts their conversation. "That woman can talk all day if you let her."

"Oh, I remember." I give Blaze a quick hug, relaxing as he reciprocates. He's always been an amazing hugger.

"Hey, uh—I know this sounds dumb, but do I look okay?" Blaze wipes his hands on his pants. When he steps back, I realize he looks a bit nervous.

"As handsome as ever." I beam up at him. And I mean it. His blue polo makes his eyes stand out, and his blond hair is pulled up into a bun. "You look classy."

Blaze lets out a breath. "Okay, cool. Cool cool cool." He cracks his knuckles, looking out over the patio.

People are milling about, enjoying mimosas and the warmth from the sun. There are tennis courts off to one side, and I smile when I look at them.

"Hey, remember when I'd beat your ass at tennis?" I elbow him, and I watch him relax a bit at the distraction.

"Yeah, until I had my growth spurt and started practicing consistently." He snickers. "You always insisted on one more game, but you never won."

"Hey! I won a couple times when we were older."

"Yeah, because he let you."

I spin around to glare at Dominic. He's standing a few feet away, with a relieved-looking Xander beside him. Everly is nowhere to be seen.

"You could always beat Brooke, though." Alexander loops his arms through mine.

"Because I'm fucking tiny, you assholes."

We turn to find Brooke descending the steps. She's in a sea green sundress with little white flowers embroidered on it. She's always been short, but seeing her next to the guys makes her look so small.

When she sees me, her jaw drops. "Oh my god, Sophia! It's been so long." Flying down the rest of the steps, she plows into me.

"Hey, beautiful." I squeeze her before holding her at arm's length to get a good look at her. She's only two years younger than Xander, but she didn't hang out with us too much. Still, I remember the spark of joy that was always in her eyes—the one that's currently missing. "How've you been?"

"Oh, just fine." She grins at me, but her smile doesn't reach her soft brown eyes. "I moved back in with mum for a bit, but I'm about ready to go home. She's driving me crazy."

"You're sure?" Xander's tone is soft. He steps forward to put a hand on her arm.

It warms my heart. He's always been there for his little sister, no matter what.

"I'm positive. At this point, she's hurting me more than she's helping." Fiddling with the edge of her dress, she turns back to me. "Come get some mimosas with me. I want to hear about how you've been."

Before I can say anything, she's pulling me away. When I glance back at the guys, I notice that all three of them look concerned. Odd.

But I don't pry. If she wants to tell me what's going on, she will. Instead, I answer all her questions, telling her what I've been up to for the past five years. For some reason, Brooke has always felt safe. Like home. Opening up to her doesn't feel embarrassing at all.

"I'm sorry everyone rejected you after your parents went bankrupt." Brooke squeezes my hand as we walk the perimeter of the perfectly-trimmed lawn. "I was so caught up in my own drama back then. And I honestly thought most of it was because Alex broke up with you."

"That was a part of it." I sigh, trying to block out the wave of emotions threatening to crush me. After all this time, I still can't think of my senior year without all the feelings that came with that time.

"Oh, Soph. I'm so sorry. And I'm so sorry Alex broke up with you. He really didn't have a choice, I promise. Our dad—" She stops talking, her eyes glossing over. Shaking her head, she says, "He loved you. Just know that, okay?"

I bite my lip. The more I hear from the people around Alexander, the more it seems like his actions are sincere. He *does* want me.

"So you two are back together?" Her eyes are hopeful, albeit void of energy and happiness. "Or are you just . . ." She shrugs.

"Just what?"

"I dunno. Alex doesn't really date anymore. He usually has some girl on his arm to keep mum from badgering him too much. But I haven't seen him in a real relationship in years."

"Oh. Well, uh, I'm not really sure what we are. So I guess just a fling or whatever."

So much for his actions being sincere.

Brooke nods, taking my hand in hers. "I was hoping it was something more with you two. You make him less grumpy."

I snort at that, and we head back to the tables. Food has been served, and my stomach is growling.

Spotting the guys, we make our way to their table. But something stops me, a burning feeling on the back of my neck.

I turn to find Tristan standing next to Everly's chair, holding a conversation with her. But he's staring at me.

Shivering, I turn away. It's odd that he's here, considering his rivalry with Xander. But I suppose the Hendricks' lives have always been intertwined with the Goodwin's. The elite have a way of sticking together.

Thankfully, the food is a good distraction. And we keep the conversation light, joking and remembering the good times we had as kids.

Blaze is in the middle of telling a story about pulling a prank on Brooke when I feel a strong hand gripping my shoulder.

Alexander shoots out of his seat next to me, his whole body stiff. "Fuck off, Tristan."

"Actually, I'd like to make a little deal with you, Hendricks." Tristan's grip tightens on my shoulder when I try to squirm away.

"What?" There's nothing but disgust in Alexander's voice as he glares daggers at Tristan.

"How about a little tennis? I'd love to whoop your ass in front of all your mother's friends."

Rolling his eyes, Xander steps forward. He's a few inches taller than Tristan, but his intimidation tactics don't seem to be working. "Or you could just fuck off."

"Hear me out." Tristan's voice is dripping with mock friendliness, and it makes me shiver. "If I win, I get to take your pretty little girlfriend on a date. I'm sure I can show her a better time than you can. If I lose, I'll leave this sorry excuse for a brunch so you can enjoy your morning in peace."

Rage bubbles into my throat. "I'm not anyone's *pretty little girlfriend*. And neither of you can throw me around like a fucking toy." I stand to face Tristan head on, but he shoves me back down into my chair.

At that, Dominic stands, throwing his napkin on the table. But Xander moves first, ripping Tristan's hand off me and twisting his arm behind his back.

"Touch her again, and you'll regret it," Alexander growls.

"Boys! What's going on?" Everly's voice cuts through the tension in the air. She comes to stand in front of Xander and Tristan, a frown on her face.

"Oh, I was just challenging Alex here to a friendly game of tennis. He didn't seem too happy about it." Tristan flashes her a charming smile as Xander releases him. "Probably afraid he'll lose."

"Oh, seriously, Alex? Just play the game. No need for things to get violent."

Xander starts to protest, but Everly holds up her hand. "Go. It'll be fun to see. I haven't watched you play in quite some time."

With a quick glance to me, Alexander storms off, Tristan following him.

Everly laughs, turning to everyone else. "Boys will be boys."

I rub my shoulder. Tristan's grip was hard and rough, and it's a bit sore.

"Are you all right?" Dominic's voice is quiet as he kneels next to me. His jaw is set, and I can see fury burning behind his eyes. But his touch is gentle as he puts a hand on my arm.

"Just pissed." I shake my head. "Who the fuck does Tristan think he is? I'm not an object, and Xander doesn't own me."

"That's not a concept misogynists can grasp," Brooke says. The bitterness in her voice surprises me. My eyes follow her when she stands up and heads back up the stairs to the house.

Blaze stands, also watching her.

"Don't you dare," Dominic says. He catches his brother's gaze, and they stare at each other for a moment, having a silent conversation.

When Blaze sits back down, his fists are clenched.

I move to the fence surrounding the tennis court, watching as Tristan serves. The ball bounces once before Xander hits it back, and I watch as it bounces in an unexpected direction. Tristan almost misses, but course corrects at the last possible section.

I bite my lip. Even if Tristan wins, I'm not going on a date with him. But I sure as hell still want him to lose.

Tristan scores the first point, and I can feel irritation creeping up inside of me.

Come on, Xander.

"So he's back to you, huh?"

I tense at Vanessa's voice. Of course. Why am I even surprised she was invited, too? "Excuse me?"

"Alex, of course." She comes to stand next to me, her light perfume drifting to my nostrils. "You're his latest whore."

"I'm not a whore, Vanessa."

She lets out a judgmental hum before waving at Xander and blowing him a kiss. "This is just what he does, honey. He plays with a girl for a few weeks, has her over for a couple weekends, and when he's bored, he ghosts her."

Taking a deep breath to calm my boiling nerves, I turn to her. "Speaking from experience, huh?" My voice comes out cool and even.

Vanessa's jaw drops, and she narrows her eyes. "Just you wait and see, you bitch." Then she huffs off, her dark hair bouncing off her shoulders.

She may look perfect, but on the inside, she's rotten.

I turn back just in time to see Xander score.

"You've got this, Alex," Blaze shouts as he comes to stand next to me. Then he murmurs, "What the fuck did she want?"

"Nothing," I mumble. I have no desire to talk about Alexander right now. I don't want Vanessa's words to be confirmed.

Tristan almost scores, but ends up slamming the ball straight into the net.

"Thank god," I say, and Blaze chuckles.

"Don't want to go on a date with the devil's spawn?"

"Blaze, let's be real. I came here *with* the devil's spawn. Tristan is something far worse."

He laughs, his eyes following as Tristan and Xander hit the ball back and forth.

It's nerve-wracking for sure, but after realizing that I very well might just be one of Alexander's *whores,* I kind of want both of them to lose.

Too bad that's not how the game works.

While Tristan and Xander battle for the next point, my mind battles with itself.

Vanessa's words are worth less than shit.

But she's been around Xander more over the past few years.

And Brooke said he doesn't do long-term relationships anymore.

But Dominic says he's always treated you differently.

But that was five years ago. We've all grown up.

Sure, I could just ask Alexander. But how do I do that without betraying the fact that I *want* him to want me? Forever. He's always had a dark side, and if it's come back out to play, I don't want to give him one more thing that he can use to manipulate me.

And I'm also not sure I'll trust the words that leave his mouth. Even if it's what I want to hear.

Finally, Alexander scores, and relief floods me. Tristan looks ready to explode, but he holds it together. There are lots of people watching.

Alexander tosses his racket onto a bench, exiting the fence and jogging over to me. With everyone's eyes on us, he takes me into his arms and kisses me. His sweaty skin sticks to mine as he pulls away.

"I was worried there at first," Blaze says, elbowing him. "Tristan got you good at the beginning."

"You really think I'd let Tristan have the satisfaction of beating me? Or that I'd let him think he had a chance to get a date in with Sophia?"

"I wouldn't've gone," I growl.

"Damn right. Over my dead fucking body."

When I dated Tristan in high school, he was a complete asshole. Not only did Xander help me get away from him, but he made sure Tristan stayed away from me after we broke up.

Even though I'm irritated at this whole situation, Xander's protectiveness fills me with a warm and fuzzy feeling. I'd love to say that it's just nostalgia, but it's not. I *like* that he hates the thought of me being with Tristan. It means there's hope that he still wants me the way he wanted me years ago.

And *not* just as another pretty girl.

"Leave," Xander spits out, glaring at Tristan.

Thankfully, he leaves without protest, just as he promised.

Xander keeps me by his side for the rest of the brunch. Blaze disappears for a while, and then reappears a couple minutes before Brooke does. Her eyes are a little red and puffy, but she pretends to be fine, laughing and joking with the rest of us.

And avoiding Blaze like the plague.

Curiosity pricks at me, but I ignore it. Brooke's life is hers, and I'm not going to pry. Being too invasive of her personal life and pushing her away is the last thing I want.

Looking around at all my old friends circled around our table, chatting and making fun, my heart squeezes. I've missed them all so much. And dammit, I don't want to push *any* of them away. I want them all back in my life. Forever.

Blaze's deep laughs. Dominic's calculating, serious expressions. Brooke's sweetness and compassion. And Xander—all of Xander.

They used to be mine. And I almost didn't survive when I lost them.

As people start leaving, I notice Everly staring at me. No—that's not accurate. *Glaring.* I give her a patronizing smile and turn away, snaking an arm around Xander's waist.

He smiles down at me with satisfaction, whispering in my ear, "Good to know you still like pissing off my mother."

"Of course I do." I kiss him on the cheek before smirking at Everly.

"God, it makes me want to fuck you even more. When we're home, I'm going to rip this little thing off of you, tie you to the bed, and slam you into the mattress until we both pass out."

My cheeks heat, and I hope his voice is quiet enough that no one else hears. But Dominic is focused on his phone, and Blaze is trying—and failing—to discreetly watch Brooke as she talks to one of Everly's friends.

"Actually," Alexander says to me. "I think I'm ready now. Watching you move in this dress is pure torture."

I smile up at him, feeling heat pool between my thighs. The thought of his hands on me is exhilarating, and it's exactly what I need to distract myself from all the confusing thoughts in my head.

"Yes, please."

. . .

"I've wanted to bury my dick in you all day." Xander is standing behind me. His hands cup my breasts.

We're in his room, after he steered his car home with one hand while fingering me with the other. And now, somehow, he's managed to completely strip me down without taking off a single article of his own clothing.

I rest my head on his chest as he pinches my nipples. "All day? Didn't you enjoy battling Tristan for me?"

He stiffens, pinching my nipples harder. "Don't you dare say his name."

I smirk. I knew mentioning Tristan would set him on edge—set off his possessive side. And what I need right now is for Xander to take me, to make me his, and make him mine in the process.

"Mmm, I'm curious though. Where would he have taken me? Do you think we would've ended up back at his place?"

"Sophia," Xander growls. He's pissed.

Good.

"He may be an asshole, but you know what? He always was a good kisser."

"That's *enough*." He spins me around, forcing me to my knees. "You don't get to speak about other men that way. Only me."

His shorts are unzipped in a second, and his hard cock taunts me. When he presses it against my mouth, I open, licking him.

"You're *mine,* Sophia. And only mine. The only name that will ever cross your lips is mine. You can whisper it. Moan it. Scream it. But *only mine.*"

He's taken control, holding my hair and pumping inside me until tears fall from my eyes. But I don't mind. Hell, I love it. When he picks up his pace, I can't help but moan.

I could stay in this feeling forever—of being wholly his, of being his whole world. As I watch his face, I know there's no other thought going through his head but *me.*

And I want it to stay like that forever.

"Soph." His grip on my hair tightens, and he finishes in my mouth until his cum is dripping down my chin. When he pulls out, he watches me as I swallow. But when I move to wipe my face, he catches my wrist. "*Mine.* You're mine."

I nod, my eyes wide as I look up at him. "Yours."

He hauls me to my feet, throwing me onto the bed. I try to adjust myself, but he holds me down. When I feel something soft but strong against my wrists, I let out a moan.

"I meant what I said," he grunts, tightening the rope around my wrists. "You're mine, and I intend to make sure you never forget." He keeps working with the rope, tying it to the bedframe before hovering over me.

"Xander," I breathe out, my eyes on him.

He just gives me a tender kiss, licking his cum from my chin. "I never want to let you out of my fucking sight."

With that, he moves down, his tongue finding my clit almost immediately. He doesn't hold back. He drives two fingers inside of me, curling them into one of my sweet spots. His tongue explores me, his mouth sucking on my clit.

"Oh, god, Xander," I moan, my body writhing. I pull tight against the rope binding my wrists.

How is it that I feel the most free when I give over all control to this man? When I let him do to me as he pleases?

The first orgasm hits me hard, and I can't help the screams. The second one is less intense, but he makes it last, turning his strokes against my clit feather-light.

When he pulls his fingers out of me, I whimper at the emptiness. But it's only temporary. I feel him at my entrance, just barely pressing into me.

"Do you want me to fuck you, Sophia?"

"Yes," I cry out, grinding my hips, trying to push him further into me. "Please, Xander. I want to feel you inside of me."

"You want me to fill you?" He pushes himself in just a bit more. "Claim you? Because you're mine and only mine."

I nod, panting as I look into his perfect, golden-brown eyes. "Yes, Xander. And you're mine."

His eyes darken, and he slams into me. I expect him to slow his pace, but he doesn't. Instead, he watches as my breasts bounce from the force of his thrusts. He takes me in, fucking me with all his might. One hand covers my mouth to stifle my screams. The other rests beside my head, steadying him.

It doesn't take me long to come again. My body convulses at the waves of pleasure, and soon he's grunting and burying his head in the crook of my neck.

"God, Soph." He nibbles at the soft skin of my neck. "Fuck."

We stay there, with him collapsed on top of me. I can feel Xander's heart hammering through his chest, almost like it's trying to tear out of his body and join mine.

After a few minutes, he pulls out of me and loosens the ropes. "I'm going to take a quick shower. Don't move."

I just smile at him with dazed eyes. My mind still hasn't come all the way down yet. So when he kisses my nose lightly, I just let out a small moan.

He's not even gone for a minute when I hear his phone vibrate on the bedside table. Curiosity pulls at me, and I roll over to glance at the screen.

And my stomach drops.

A text message sits on his lockscreen. Just a few words, but they tear my heart into shreds.

Vanessa: Can't wait to see you later.

The feelings creep in before I can stop them.

Used. I've been used. Played. Not even treated with basic human decency. In Alexander's eyes, I'm just a plaything.

One of his whores.

I hold back tears as I jump from bed and pull on the nearest clothes I can find. If I'm quick, maybe I can get out of here before Alexander gets out of the shower. I can call a cab, wait outside, and—

The first sob hits. It's hard enough that I fall back onto the bed, shaking.

How could he do this to me? Why?

Because he's a monster, and you've just been ignoring all the red flags.

An angry resolve fills me, and I continue throwing my things into my bag. Just as I'm grabbing my dress, I hear a startled sound from behind me.

"Soph? What are you doing?"

I wipe away my tears before turning around. "Just getting out of your way so you can get to your evening plans."

"What the hell are you talking about?" He steps forward, and I hate that my eyes linger on his muscular chest, his abs, and the way his towel hugs his hips and thighs.

"Like you don't know," I snap, scrunching up my dress in my hands. "Who am I to you, Xander? What exactly am I?"

He hesitates, moving to stand by his dresser. Closer to me, but still far enough away that I don't try to back away.

"What do you want from me, Alexander?"

"I don't think you're ready for the answer to that, little bird."

"Why, because you know I hate being used? Being treated like a toy? You don't own me, and I won't let you use me as your arm candy."

He smirks. "The sex is pretty good, too."

I yell in frustration. This is *not* the time for him to be all witty. "So that's it. That's all I am to you. A pretty girl for appearance and a good fuck."

He shrugs, leaning against his dresser. "Maybe. But that doesn't sound like what you want."

Maybe.

My heart just about breaks.

Scratch that—it never healed from last time.

My heart fucking shatters.

"Don't you dare turn this around on me, Xander." I throw my dress at him, but he catches it easily.

He lifts the fabric up to his nose. "Smells like you. Delicious. Perfect."

"Seriously?" I step forward and snatch it away from him. "What am I to you? What the fuck do you want? Do you even care about me a bit?"

An arm wraps around my waist, and he pulls me into him. My body is flush with his, his hand pressing on the small of my back. One of his fingers comes up against my chin, pushing it up until I'm forced to look at him.

His wet hair is tangled, his chiseled jawline set. He smells amazing. Intoxicating. Addictive. And those brown eyes, soft and hard at the same time, are full of passion and lust and something else.

"Before getting in my face about what I want, you need to figure out what *you* want, Sophia." His hand wraps around the back of my neck, pulling me closer until my lips brush against his.

When he kisses me, my mind goes blank. All I can focus on is Xander, his presence, his scent, the way he bites my bottom lip.

When he pulls away, I moan, aching for more. But he runs a hand through my hair. "What do you want, Sophia?"

I hesitate.

I want Alexander. I do. I really, *really* do. But I want all of him—not just a fling. I want security. I want to know that he'll never leave me again.

And it doesn't matter if he tells me nothing will ever come between us again. I don't think I can believe him.

Not after that text from Vanessa.

I open my mouth to tell him that. To end us. To tell him that I want him, but that I don't think I can ever trust him.

But the words don't come out.

A familiar feeling creeps into my gut—the feeling I had right after Alexander left me sobbing behind our high school.

I told him I loved him, and he told me we were over.

I can't—I *won't*—give him that kind of power over me again. He isn't worth the risk of vulnerability.

So I step back, shaking my head. "I don't know."

"Then it's time you figured it out, little bird."

CHAPTER 8

Sophia

Xander completely ghosts me.

I don't hear from him at all on Sunday, and I don't expect him to pick me up for work on Monday morning.

Still, the disappointment stings as I walk to work alone in the dark of the morning.

Tuesday is the same.

No showing up at the coffee shop. No calls. Not a single text.

A part of me is relieved. My life is back to normal. Just work, hanging out with Rachel and Victoria, my talks with Lissa, and plowing away at my client's novel.

But I'm very obviously not okay, and Lissa has been shooting me concerned looks all week. Even Brent picks up on it the second he sees me Monday morning.

I'm supposed to figure out what I want. The problem is, I already know that. I just don't know how to express it.

Or, to be perfectly honest, I don't trust Alexander enough to put all my cards on the table.

Every night, my mind has been filled with Brooke's and Vanessa's words.

He doesn't really date anymore. He only does flings. And he just goes from one girl to the next, using them up until he gets bored.

And then he ghosts them.

Just like he's ghosting me.

But his words still haunt me. *I'm not losing you again, Soph.*

Did he mean it? Or did he know those were the magic words that would make me fall into his lap?

Alexander played with me and then dropped me the second I got too inconvenient.

Just like last time.

Just like Vanessa predicted.

And I only have myself to blame, for falling into a demon's trap and playing his games.

Never again.

"Are you okay?" Lissa nudges me.

I snap to attention. It's Wednesday morning, and I'm at the coffee shop. Working. With a cup in my hand. "Right. Yes. Yeah, I'm fine. What am I making?" I turn, looking for the drink ticket on the counter.

"Babe, do you need to take a minute? Do you need to talk? You haven't been yourself the past couple of days."

I sigh, finishing the coffee in my hands. I've already told her about my fight with Alexander, and about him ghosting me. She knows how I feel, and she knows how scared I am.

And, according to her, Alexander is a bottom-feeding asshole who should rot in hell.

"I'm fine," I say, plastering on my best fake smile. "Just a lot on my mind."

"Soph, just let him go. I know you want this to work, but how can you trust him? He's a jerk. And you deserve better."

The front door opens and Brent breezes in, a smile on his face. He's been showing up early for a while now, and I'm proud of him. I'm sure his boss is happy about it, too.

"Morning, Brent!" Lissa gives him a wave before nudging me and whispering, "There's a perfect distraction for you."

"Shut *up*, Lissa." My cheeks redden.

"No. You need to see other people. *He* is. Brent, are you free tonight? Can you take this shell of a human being out on a date for me?" Lissa shoves me forward until I bump into the counter.

My eyes widen as I glance at Brent. A mixture of hope and caution swirls in his eyes.

"Sophia, if you'd like, I'd be honored to take you on a date." His voice is gentle, his eyes kind. "Even if it's just as friends. If it'll help you get your mind off of whatever's bothering you, I'll do anything to help."

Anything.

Anything.

Jesus. Maybe Lissa is right. Why let Alexander play with my heart and manipulate me when Brent is willing to do anything to make me happy?

Fuck Alexander. Fuck his stupid face, and fuck his stupid games.

"I think I'd like that, Brent." I force myself to look up at him.

He's beaming—absolutely beaming.

"Uh, I'll make your coffee."

While I fumble with a cup, Lissa rings him out.

. . .

"You look beautiful."

Brent is standing on the front porch, a small bouquet of flowers in his hands. His eyes fill with awe as he takes in my lightly-curled hair and yellow sundress.

"Th-thanks. You didn't have to get me flowers." I let him inside and take the bouquet, inhaling the sweet aromas.

"I wanted to." Brent smiles, leaning in and kissing me on the cheek.

I fight the urge to go completely stiff, clutching the stems of the flowers too tightly instead. "Just let me put these in water real quick."

He nods, and I disappear into the kitchen.

I don't know why I was expecting Brent to be a nervous mess. Seeing him standing on the porch with his shoulders back surprised me. He's calm, even charming. Just like—

No. Don't you dare think about him right now.

I shove the flowers into a jar with water and head back out. "Ready?"

He offers me his arm. "I made us reservations at one of my favorite restaurants. I think you'll like it. You love reading, right?"

"I do, yeah." My heart warms. He remembered? Or did Lissa remind him at some point today?

The drive only takes 15 minutes, and then we're parked in front of an older brick building. Diners sit on the patio under umbrellas, chatting and eating delicious-looking food.

When we get inside, I gasp. Beautiful chandeliers hang from the ceiling, shining on white tablecloths and pristine wine glasses. But that's not what I care about.

I care about the walls, covered in bookshelves all the way to the ceiling. People stroll on the floors above us, either looking at all the books or staring down into the dining room.

"Brent, this is beautiful," I say. Even as a hostess leads us to our table, I can't take my eyes off the shelves bursting with books, new and old.

"I thought you might like it. I came here with my grandmother a lot when I was younger." Brent pulls out my chair for me and helps me get settled.

"I can't believe I never knew this place existed." I beam at Brent. "This was so thoughtful of you."

He shrugs. "I can't take all the credit."

Giggling, I say, "Lissa told you what I like?"

Brent nods, reaching across the table to take my wrist in his. "I want you to enjoy yourself tonight. Don't worry about the prices of anything. Just forget about whatever's bugging you, okay?"

"Oh—you don't have to pay. I'm perfectly fine with splitting the bill." Sure, the cost of one meal here could probably buy me groceries for a week. But I make my own money, dammit. And I have no desire to be financially dependent on a man.

"No, please. Let me. I have a real job. I don't mind."

"A real job." I can already feel my stomach twisting. Seriously? I work my ass off every day. "Food service jobs *are* real jobs."

"Right, of course. You know what I mean. It just doesn't pay well, that's all. Not that I mind. I don't, I swear. I honestly believe the man in a relationship should provide financially. Women are better at other things."

Great. How did I attract a fucking misogynist?

Alexander might be an asshole, but he hasn't tried to control my career or my finances. On the contrary, when he saw that I was writing a book, he was happy for me. Proud of me.

When he saw I was in over my head, he didn't tell me I was incapable. He did what he could to support me without getting in my way.

Still, the jerk thinks he owns you.

And you fucking like it, Sophia.

I give Brent a polite smile. This isn't the place for my inner feminist to tear him to shreds, and I don't have the energy tonight. Instead, I do as he says and order one of the most expensive items on the menu.

We chat while waiting for our food. He tells me a bit more about his grandmother. She loved poetry the most, and she left Brent her collection when she passed.

I let him in on my family a bit—leaving out the parts in which Francis Hendricks completely ruined my father.

"So, what's going on with you and that guy from the coffee shop?" Brent asks, sipping his wine.

For a moment, I just stare at him—because *Brent* is the guy from the coffee shop, in my mind. "Oh, Alexander? It's complicated. I'm not really sure what we are."

"He seems a bit immature. But I suppose he's still young."

"He's my age." I shrug. I almost forgot that Brent is in his early thirties. "We dated in high school."

"Oof. Tough competition. He already knows you." He winks, and I have to hide my cringe.

First Tristan, and now Brent. Why do men think women are something to be won? At least Alexander doesn't—but that's because he's practically forcing me into a relationship.

Except now he's giving me a choice?

I wonder what would happen if I say I don't want to be with him.

"Earth to Sophia. You in there?" Brent waves his hand in front of my eyes.

"Sorry. I've just had a lot on my mind lately. Oh look, our food." I lean back as a pretty blonde waitress slides my plate in front of me.

"Enjoy," she says, smiling at us both.

When Brent winks at her, I throw out the entire idea of being with him. Why would he do that? Gross.

I keep the rest of our conversation as un-intimate as I possibly can, telling him about my day and asking him boring questions about his job. Soon enough, we're getting back into his car.

Once we're on our way, I shoot a text to the group chat with Rachel and Victoria. We always update each other on our whereabouts when we're going on a date with a new guy.

"Texting your other boyfriend?" Brent says jokingly, but I catch a hint of jealousy.

"Oh, no, just a few friends. They're curious about how the date went. I was just telling them to shut up."

"So you told your friends about me."

Fuck.

Brent takes it as a hint, and his hand slides onto my leg.

Fuck fuck fuck.

"I just told them I had a date," I say lightly, trying not to squirm. Then I send another text.

Why is it that when Alexander touches me, it completely unravels me, but when Brent does it, I want to cut his hand off?

Thankfully, the rest of the drive is spent silently listening to the classical music coming from the radio. I wonder if he did that as a romantic touch, or if that's what he listens to on the regular.

When he pulls up in front of my house, my heart practically stops.

Across the street is a sleek, gray car that's all too familiar. And it's empty.

"Well, thank you so much for dinner. The restaurant was beautiful."

"Not as beautiful as you, Sophia."

"Oh, I don't know about that. But thanks." I fumble with the car door.

"I'll walk you to your house. It's getting dark out, and this isn't the best neighborhood."

It's as safe as anywhere else, you classist fuck.

Smiling, I keep as much distance as possible between us as we head up the sidewalk. When we hit the top of the porch steps, I reach into my purse for my keys.

Come on, guys.

"Listen, Sophia, tonight has been amazing." Brent takes my hand, pulling me close to him. An arm wraps around my waist. "Your smile lights up my whole world."

Gross.

Finally, the front door swings open. Light floods the porch as Victoria and Rachel run out.

"Hey beautiful!" Victoria says. "We've been waiting for you to get home."

"Oh, hey there . . . Uh, which one is this, Soph?" Rachel frowns at Brent, even though she knows exactly who he is.

"Hmm, he's too short to be Alexander."

Brent goes stiff, but he doesn't let me go. "Ladies, could you give us a minute?"

Victoria and Rachel both glance at me, and then each other.

"Actually," Victoria says, "We have something we really need Sophia for. So if you could—"

"*Give us a minute.*"

"I don't think so," a deep voice says.

A tall figure steps into the doorframe, and Victoria and Rachel shrink back, whispering.

"Xander, what are you doing here?" It comes out startled, even though I meant for it to come off irritated.

He ignores me, his cool glare settling on Brent. "Get your hands off of her before I break you in two."

Brent does the opposite, tightening his arm around my waist. "Last time I checked, you don't own her."

"Last time I checked, neither do you, asshole."

I try to squirm away from Brent. "I really would like you to let me go."

Frustration flashes through his eyes, but he releases me.

Pulling me behind him, Alexander murmurs, "Get inside."

But I stay exactly where I am, watching as he grabs Brent by the collar and slams his fist into his face. "Touch her again, and you'll wish you'd never been born, asshole. Now fuck off."

I should be surprised. Shocked. Horrified, even.

But instead, watching as blood trickles from Brent's nose, I have to work to keep my relieved smile at bay.

I watch as he stalks to his car and slams the door shut with such force it echoes in between the houses.

"Looks like you dodged a bullet," Victoria mutters from behind me.

Turning, I hug her. "Thanks for coming to my rescue. I'm glad you got my text."

"Girlfriend, we've got you." Rachel wraps her arms around both of us. "That creep was totally gonna try to kiss you."

Alexander lets out a low growl. He's still facing the street, watching Brent pull out and speed down the street.

"What's he doing here?" I whisper to the girls.

Rachel shrugs. "Has a question to ask you."

Right, because it may be my choice, but it'll definitely be on his terms.

Rolling my eyes, I stalk inside and run up the stairs to my room. I can't get rid of the feeling of Brent's hands on me. My skin crawls, like I need to shower and scrub my whole body until it's bleeding.

I throw on some sweatpants under my dress and rummage through my dresser for a shirt.

"Don't you dare take that dress off." Alexander's voice is low as he steps into my room and shuts the door.

"Just because you punched a guy for me doesn't mean I owe you anything. Fuck off."

He flips me around and pins me against my dresser. My back digs into the handles. Maybe on a different day, I'd enjoy this. But tonight, his closeness—his downright *invasion* of my personal space—makes me want to throw up.

"What the hell were you doing, going on a date with him?"

I stay silent, turning my head and looking away. At anything but him.

"Answer me, little bird."

"Just let me get changed."

"You think I'm going to let you remember this dress as the one you wore out on a date with *him?* Not a chance. You're going to remember this dress as the one you wore while I fucked you until you screamed for the whole house to hear."

"Please don't touch me," I say in a soft, small voice. I hate that that's how I sound. I'm angry, not scared. I can handle myself. But still, I sound like a cornered child about to start crying.

Xander is off me in a split second, putting enough distance between us that I feel like I can breathe.

"Turn around so I can finish changing."

He obeys silently, to my surprise.

Then again, Xander always stopped when I told him to—not that I did very often.

I change quickly and then lower myself onto my bed. "I wasn't sure if I was going to hear from you again."

"Can I turn around?"

"Yes."

He does, shoving his hands into his pockets. "This is what you wanted, isn't it? A choice. And I gave you space to make one. Have you decided?"

"I have."

He waits.

But I don't answer.

"Sophia."

"I need Blaze's number."

Xander's nostrils flare. He came here to see if I want him or not, and I ask him for another man's number. Who knows what he's thinking right now.

"Why the fuck would I give it to you?"

"You want an answer from me."

"Blaze isn't involved in this," Xander growls.

"He is to me. I need to talk to him."

"Why?" His fists are clenched in his pockets.

"Just give me his number and go. Meet me in the park tomorrow at five." I stand, grabbing my phone and pulling up a blank contact profile.

Xander grunts, snatching my phone and typing in a number before handing it back. He turns to go without a word.

"Xander."

He pauses. One of his hands grips the doorframe as he spins around. Even in the dim lighting of my bedroom, I can see the fury swimming in his eyes.

"Thank you."

His face softens, just for a moment. Then he's standing in front of me, so close we're almost touching—almost. "I want to be very clear about something, Sophia. I don't give a fuck what you tell me your decision is tomorrow. No matter what, if he gives you trouble again, you call me. I don't care how trivial it is. If he makes you even the slightest bit uncomfortable, I'll fucking kill him."

The smile on my lips is entirely involuntary. I hate that I love how protective Xander is. "I know."

He nods, stepping back. "Goodnight."

I watch as he descends the stairs, and then I lock myself in my bedroom.

I have a call to make.

CHAPTER 9

Sophia

I talk to Blaze for two hours. He's patient with me as I pick his brain, pulling as much information out of him as I can.

When I finally hang up, sleep comes easily. Until it doesn't.

I wake to a dark, broad figure looming over me. My hands are tied, and when I try to scream, a hand clamps over my mouth.

I try to knee the man on top of me, kicking and squirming, but it's all in vain.

"Shut up, Sophia. You're only making this harder on yourself."

I freeze at the voice.

No. No, no, no. What's Tristan doing in my house?

"That's right—you should be *very* afraid." His hand wraps around my throat, squeezing too tightly.

"Tris-" I choke out, struggling against the ropes binding my wrists.

He lets up a little, and I gasp in a breath.

"What the hell—"

He slaps me, and the stinging pain across my cheeks shocks me into silence.

"I'll keep this simple so your little brain can keep up." A finger traces down my cheek. "You have my number one enemy wrapped around your finger. Tomorrow, when you have your little meetup to chat, you're going to get back together with him. Do you understand?"

"How did you—"

"I know everything, Sophia. *Everything.* So tomorrow, you tell him yes. You'll be his stupid little girlfriend, and you'll sleep in his bed, and you'll make him fall harder than he ever has before. And when the timing is right, you're going to fucking break him."

"W-what? No. Why would I do that?"

He slaps me again, and I grit my teeth to stop a whimper from escaping. Instead, I stay perfectly still and glare up at his dark figure.

"I have the power to completely destroy the entire Hendricks family. To take Alexander away from you, for life. To break poor little Brooke's heart all over again. All I have to do is send one simple message to the local authorities. Is that what you'd like?"

"You're bluffing." I try to knee him again, but he just clamps his legs around my sides and squeezes—hard.

"Is that a chance you want to take?" He leans in close, until we share the same air.

My breath catches. "What do you have on him?"

Tristan lets out a low chuckle. "That's need-to-know, my dear. And—well, you don't. You'll do exactly what I want you to."

"And why do you think that?" I snap. Against my better judgment, I start struggling under him again.

"Because you're still in love with him."

His words are like another slap to the face. I freeze, my chest heaving, my eyes wide.

Tristan just laughs. "Deny it all you want. Hell, you can even lie to yourself if it helps you sleep at night. But I know the truth. You're just as desperate to keep him as he is you."

As I shake my head, tears sting my eyes.

This can't be real.

"Let me be clear, Aswall. If you tell him about this—if you try to fuck up this plan in *any* way, I won't hesitate to sic the authorities on him. And trust me, I *will* find out. I have eyes everywhere. And you'll never see your precious Xander again."

"No, Tristan, please."

"You're going to do whatever I tell you to do. Understood?"

I nod, blinking back tears.

Before I can even try to stop him, Tristan slams his lips against mine. He bites my bottom lip until I taste blood, and then he licks the pain away.

I squirm, finally managing to knee him in the balls, even if it's not with much force. He grunts and pulls away.

"Still just as much of a brat as you used to be." He slides off of me. "Don't forget, Sophia. I'll be watching you. So keep your damn mouth shut and do what you're told."

I stare at the dark ceiling, wishing my eyes would stop producing so many damn tears.

Then he's gone, leaving only an empty, dark feeling in his wake.

As I work to free myself from the ropes, a piece of the puzzle clicks.

I remember Dominic's voice, harshly telling Xander that he's fucking with my life. There was something about Tristan, too. And Vanessa.

That's when it hits me: there's something bigger going on here than Tristan getting revenge.

And somehow, I'm caught up in the middle of it.

. . .

I stare at myself in the mirror, sorely disappointed with the reflection staring back at me.

After Tristan left, it took me forever to get out of the ropes. By the time I was free, there was no way I was going to get to sleep.

Work today was exhausting, and my shift dragged by slower than ever. Was it because I knew I was meeting Xander later? Probably. But it was still tortuous.

Now, no matter what magic I try to work with my makeup, I can't make myself look like anything other than a zombie.

Sighing, I turn away. I need to start heading to the park or I'll be late.

The thought of Tristan in my house again makes me shudder, so I make sure to lock up. Not that it'll do any good. I'm about to head down the sidewalk when I notice Xander across the street, leaning against his car.

I can't help but smile. Of course he'd pick me up.

After crossing the street, I give him a quick kiss on the cheek. He doesn't try to touch me or hold me or pin me against the car and kiss me until I'm breathless. He just gives me a small nod.

After last night, I don't blame him for having his guard up. But if he wants to have me, it's going to have to come crashing down—fast.

Once Xander left last night, I called Blaze. The conversation lasted for almost two hours while I asked him every question I could about Xander. Is he playing with me? Does he just want to hurt me for his own entertainment? Or does he actually want me?

Blaze answered all my questions without hesitation, except one. One that, unfortunately, only Xander can answer.

And it'll determine the course of the rest of our lives.

After a few minutes, I realize we're not heading to the park. "Where are you taking me?"

"You'll find out," Xander says smoothly.

I've been hoping that this little outing of ours would go without a hitch. Just a conversation—questions, answers, and a mutual agreement.

But now?

Goddammit, I'm so tired of being treated like a child. Like an object.

"Alexander Hendricks, you don't own me, so stop acting like you do. You can't just take me random places without my consent."

"Afraid I'm going to kidnap you?" He smirks.

"Xander." My voice is full of a warning: *you're on thin fucking ice.*

"We'll be there in a few minutes. Just be patient."

I let out a loud sigh, crossing my arms over my chest. *Seriously?*

When Alexander pulls into a gravel parking lot, it takes me a second to realize where we are. My hand rests over my heart as I take in the old diner standing in front of us.

A few weeks after we broke up, Xander practically kidnapped me and took me here. It was too far out of the way—and too rundown—for anyone in our social circles to run into us.

So he brought me here in secret, bought me dinner, and then kissed me out back until I was sure he was coming back to me.

I was wrong, of course.

"I have no desire to relive my memories here." My voice is shaky, and I'm ready to punch something because of it. Anything.

"I'm asking you to make new ones."

I shake my head. "No. You're not breaking my heart here again, Alexander."

"I have no intention of doing that, little bird." His hand rests on my arm, softly squeezing. "Let me get the door for you."

My skin feels cold the second his hand leaves my arm. I watch as he circles around the car. His black T-shirt is clinging to his muscles, and I hate how good he looks.

No, you don't. You fucking love it.

When he opens the car door, he holds out a hand for me. I take it, and he pulls me up—and directly into him. With such tenderness it shocks me, he wraps an arm around me and caresses my cheek with the other. His eyes lock on mine. He's looking at me in that way I can't quite figure out. Longing? Lust? Passion? All three?

The urge to kiss him hits me, but I don't. After my conversation with Blaze last night, I was practically ready to go all in. I was ready to *really* give Xander a chance.

But then Tristan had to ruin everything.

I don't know what he has on Xander, if he has anything at all. But until I know more, I have to keep my guard up. I'm not falling for Xander just to lose him again.

I press a hand onto his chest to push away, but he catches my wrist.

"Just stay like this for a moment." He leans his forehead down to rest on mine. "If this is the last time I get to hold you, I want it to last."

A breath escapes me as he closes his eyes. *This* is the Xander I remember adoring. The one who didn't hide his emotions from me.

"Xander . . ."

He hushes me, holding me closer for a second. Then he plants a lingering kiss on my forehead before releasing me. "Did you eat after work?"

I shake my head. "Had to stay late, didn't have time."

"Then let's get you some food."

Inside, Xander orders coffee, and I order a sandwich with fries. My stomach growls at the delicious smells of food.

Thankfully, it doesn't take long for my sandwich to come out, and I devour it.

When I'm halfway done, Xander clasps his hands together on top of the table. "You're killing me, Soph."

"I need a few answers before I tell you my decision."

He narrows his eyes at me but stays silent.

"And Xander, I want—I *need* you to be perfectly honest with me. I need you to trust me enough to lay all your cards out on the table."

"That's pretty rich coming from you."

"I'll trust you when you give me a reason to trust you. As of now, I haven't given you a reason not to trust me."

"How about that fuckwad Brent?"

"I went out with him because *you* ghosted me." I shoot him a glare.

His nostrils flare, and I can see him clenching his jaw. But he takes a deep breath. "Fine. What are your questions?"

"What's going on between you and Vanessa?"

His eyes flash. "Nothing that concerns you."

"That's not good enough."

He runs a hand through his dark hair. "We're . . . using each other. The appearance of being close to me is good for her public image. It's not too hard to pull off since my mother is still close with hers. And I'm keeping her somewhat close in case I need her to get close to someone else."

My stomach flips, because that *someone* had me tied up in my bed last night. "Which is why she was *so excited* to see you Saturday night?"

Xander straightens, his eyes narrowing. "You saw that text."

I nod, crossing my arms.

"Our families got together for dinner that night. She normally doesn't send texts like that. My guess is she was hoping you'd see it to make you jealous."

Drumming my fingers on the booth, I pause for a moment.

What he's saying makes sense. It lines up with what Blaze said last night—that Xander has no interest in Vanessa, as far as he knows.

Just give him a little bit of trust.

"Fine. I believe you—for now."

"What other questions do you have?" Xander still hasn't relaxed. He's moved from clasping his hands to gripping his coffee mug.

"Just one." I squirm in my seat, crossing my legs and then uncrossing them. "I need to know what your intentions are, Xander. What exactly do you want from me, and what exactly do you feel for me?"

His face goes slack for a moment before he shakes his head. "You're not ready to hear that."

"You don't get to decide what I'm ready for," I snap, pushing my plate out of the way and leaning forward. "If you want this to work, then I need complete honesty from you."

It's true. I may have heard the truth about Xander's feelings last night from Blaze, but it's not the same. Blaze isn't Xander, and he can't get into his head. I need to hear the words come from Xander's mouth.

"Fine. But I'm not doing this in here." He stands, throwing some cash onto the table. "Come with me."

I follow him silently, expecting us to get back into his car and drive somewhere he feels comfortable. But he takes my hand and leads me around the back of the diner.

My feet stop, and I pull my hand free. A weight settles on my shoulders, one that almost crushed me five years ago. "I can't."

"You can." He wraps an arm around my waist and pulls me forward until we're sheltered from sight. "Just take a deep breath and listen."

When his fingers brush across my cheek, pushing a few strands of hair behind my ear, I shudder.

"Sophia, I've regretted leaving you every fucking day for the past five years. You're my first thought every morning, and my last thought every night. Call me crazy, I don't care. You're my deepest obsession, and I've never stopped loving you.

"I waited too long to come back to you. I know that, and I know it was stupid. One day, hopefully I'll be able to explain it to you—and to myself. Regardless, I *need* you to know, Sophia. I love you. I've always loved you. And I can't lose you again."

His arms tighten around me as tears prick my eyes.

This. This is what I've been longing for. The Xander who's fully mine, who'll do anything to make sure I know he loves me.

I just have to hope that it'll be enough to keep him by my side.

"Soph," he whispers, his head dipping down. "Soph, I'm so sorry I left you."

I look up, letting my lips brush against his. He moans, leaning in to kiss me, but I pull away.

"I want you, Xander. I do. But I also want peace. And happiness. And loyalty. And if I can't find those things with you, don't expect me to stay. Your mother is a bitch, and I know we'll face other obstacles. If I get *any* hint that you're going to drop me again when things get too inconvenient, don't expect me to wait around for the other shoe to drop. I'll leave first."

"I won't," he murmurs into my ear. "I won't leave you. Never again. You're mine, and I won't lose you again."

It's all I need to hear. My lips find his, and he pins me against the wall as we devour each other. My passion crashes against his, like waves against a boulder. When he finally releases my lips, it's only to pick me up.

As soon as my back hits the wall again, I wrap my legs around his waist. He lets out a low groan as he moves to my neck. He sucks my tender skin hard enough to bruise, but I don't even care. I want the whole world to know I'm his.

One of his hands slides down in between us, fumbling with his pants. "I need you, Sophia. Now."

I whimper as I feel his fingers underneath my dress, yanking my panties to the side.

"God, you're already soaked." Still, he drives two fingers inside of me, his thumb finding my clit. "For me. Only for me."

"Only for you," I whisper. My whole body is shaking.

He pulls out his fingers. When he places them in front of my lips, I open without question and suck myself off his skin.

"I couldn't stop thinking about you ever since Saturday." He positions himself at my entrance and slides in slowly. "Being without you is a special kind of torture."

I moan as he fills me. It's like this is our first time. Every nerve in my body is on fire, and his touch sets off fireworks underneath my skin.

He moves inside of me slowly, enjoying every second. When his thumb finds my clit again, my whole body goes rigid with pleasure.

My hips meet each of his thrusts, and I grip his arms as he drives into me. I can already feel the buildup in my body. So I kiss him, biting his bottom lip until he groans.

As my mind and body come completely undone, I bury my face into the crook of his neck. A cry rips through me. Even when I start writhing and clutching at his shirt, he doesn't slow down. He just kisses me again, driving me into the wall. Then he swears, squeezing my ass as I feel him release inside of me.

I cling to him as he slowly kisses my neck.

"I love you, Sophia," he whispers against my skin.

I tighten my hold on him. I might not be ready to say the words back, but we've taken a step in the right direction.

Xander is mine again, really mine. And he's not going to let me go.

With time, I'll learn to trust him again.

But for now, I have what I want. And I'm not going to waste a single second.

CHAPTER 10

Alexander

"You're a stupid fuck, you know that?" Dominic is standing over his desk, giving me his signature glare.

His office at Grayson Security is fairly sparse. Minus some artwork that, I must say, doesn't suit him at all.

"She'll be fine." I lean back in one of the cushy chairs he has for his clients. Crossing my legs and resting my ankle on my knee, I say, "And she's stronger than you think."

"No thanks to you."

Dominic is more agitated than normal. Something else is bothering him, other than the clusterfuck of my life. I file away that thought for later. Because right now, Dominic has a one track mind.

Unfortunately, all of his focus is on me.

"You couldn't just wait a couple more months?" Dominic growls.

I avoid his gaze.

To be honest, it'd always been my intention to wait until we were in the clear. The last thing I want is to put her in any danger.

I thought I could satisfy myself by seeing Sophia every morning at the coffee shop. But instead of giving me any morsel of satisfaction, it made me want her more.

And when I saw that asshole Brent eyeing her up, I lost all self control.

"She wasn't even a blip on Tristan's radar before you barged back into her life." Dominic is pacing now. "Now she has a huge fucking target on her back."

"I'll keep her safe."

"How?" Dominic yells, whirling around and focusing that glare of his on me.

I almost yell back, but I stop myself. Because, goddammit, he's right. I fucked up—big time.

Normally, someone else being protective of Sophia would piss me off. But Dom and Blaze were her friends in high school, too. We were all close, and the Graysons are like brothers to me.

They're possibly the only other people on this godforsaken planet I'd trust Sophia's safety with. Or Brooke's, but I'm still holding out hope that we'll come out of this without her getting any more involved than she already is.

"How, Alex?" Dominic steps forward, his hands balled into fists at his side. "How the *fuck* are you going to keep her safe?"

I plaster on a grin, placing my hands behind my head. "I happen to have the best security company on the east coast on retainer."

Dominic's left eye twitches, but he doesn't tell me off. No, he won't. Can't. No matter how stoic he may try to appear, I know him too well. And he cares too much about Soph's safety.

"I'll arrange to have someone keep an eye on her." He runs a hand through his hair. "Fuck, Alex."

"I'm not going to let anything happen to her."

"You can't promise that. This guy is a monster." Gesturing to the open files on his desk, Dominic shakes his head. "Ten confirmed kills. God knows how many more he's hiding. Tristan isn't afraid of doing his own dirty work, and he's ruthless."

"Which is why we're going to take him down. Both of them. I promise, Dom."

He plops down into his chair, and for a second, his facade of seriousness and control disappears. His exhaustion slips through, along with a sickening amount of worry.

For Soph, for humanity in general, and for whatever else is on his mind.

Recently, Tristan has taken charge of his family's business, with his father's strict supervision. They handle cybersecurity, but we've suspected for years that it's just a front.

Then his new partner slipped up, and our suspicions were confirmed. The Goodwins do business in too many unethical, slimy ways.

Covering up the one percent's messes and crimes.

Silencing possible threats to deadly secrets.

Drug trafficking.

But that wasn't even the worst part. The worst part was that Tristan's partner in crime was none other than my little sister's fucking fiancé.

Originally, we weren't going to do anything except turn them over to the FBI. But, as it turns out, being a senator's grandson practically gives you goddamn immunity in this country. Lucky bitches.

There's a knock on the door. Felix slips in, holding a tablet in his hands. His face is grim.

"Did you get anything else off the hard drive?"

"Unfortunately, yes." Felix lowers his eyes to the ground. "This isn't good, guys. I've got a list of about fifty names—almost all female, some androgynous."

"That's all?" Dominic drums his fingers on the desk.

"The names repeat every so often. With dollar amounts."

"Jesus Christ," I murmur.

"Whatever Tristan has David in charge of, it's not the usual shit. We've got their books, but not for what we thought we'd find. Guys, this is—this is bad."

Felix is gripping the tablet so hard I'm worried it's going to break. And without even looking at Dom, I can feel the tension rolling off of him. He's always had a soft spot for kids.

I fight the urge to kidnap Sophia and get her the hell out of here. To keep her in some secluded cabin in the middle of nowhere until I know she'll be safe.

"God, I'm such an idiot." I rub my hands over my face, and Dominic grunts in response.

Felix stays silent, thankfully.

"We need to figure out how to get ahead of them," Dominic says. "And then stop them for fucking good."

"Or we could just kill them," I say, glancing at my watch.

"No. If they're involved in human trafficking, killing them isn't enough. I need to make sure their whole operation is destroyed."

Good point.

I nod, glancing at Felix. "Does Blaze know?"

"I came here as soon as I looked over the list. My team is still going through the rest of the drive, so it may be a while before we have the whole picture."

Dominic gives him a curt nod, and Felix leaves.

"On second thought," I say, "I think I'll ask Sophia to move in with me."

· · ·

When Sophia opens the front door, her eyes widen.

"Alexander." She tugs at the sleeves of her hoodie, avoiding my gaze. Her eyes are puffy and bloodshot.

My heart stops for a moment. "What happened?" Shoving my way in, I pull her into my arms. "Are you okay?"

"What? Yeah, I—I'm fine. Just had a bad day, that's all."

Earlier today, Sophia texted me to let me know she was taking the day off work because of a stomachache. I missed driving her. But now it won't matter. I'm not leaving this house until Sophia comes with me.

"Are you feeling better?" I plant a kiss on her forehead, inhaling her sweet floral scent.

"Yeah." Squirming away, she steps back. "Uh, what are you doing here?"

I open my mouth but then slam it shut.

On my way here, there was only one thing on my mind: keep Sophia safe. The idea of stealing her away to the middle of nowhere still lingers in the back of my mind. But I can't leave, not now.

There are two scumbags who we need to take down first.

I take in Sophia's disheveled state. She's emotionally vulnerable right now, which could be an advantage to me. But even if I ask her to come stay with me, I know she'll say no.

The only option is force. She'll resent me, but she'll be alive.

"Look, I have stuff to do." She's wringing her hands and backing away.

I narrow my eyes. No matter what she tries to hide from me, I've always been able to read her like a fucking book. And she's hiding something from me. "What's going on?"

"N-nothing. I'm just tired, that's all. Didn't sleep well."

I step forward, just for her to stumble back. "Don't lie to me, little bird. You couldn't get enough of me yesterday, and now it's like you're afraid of me."

She runs a hand through her beautifully light hair and closes her eyes.

"Did Dominic say something to you?"

That fucker. He's one of the only people who knows the truth about what I did six months ago. If he told Sophia to keep her away from me, I'll fucking kill him.

"Dominic? No. It—I . . ." She shakes her head.

"Sophia," I growl.

That's when I notice them—the tears in her eyes, just beginning to well up.

What the fuck is going on?

She turns, sprinting up the stairs as she sobs. *Big fucking mistake.*

I chase after her, catching her arm just as she's trying to get the door to her bedroom open. I slam her against it, pinning her arms above her head.

"Talk," I snap.

She winces at my voice, and a small part of me regrets my harsh tone. But I know Sophia. The more I give her space, the more she'll retreat into herself. Forcing this out of her is my only chance.

She sniffles but manages to glare up at me. When I don't budge, she relents. "I had the dream again."

Goddamn. I swear my kidnapping affected her more than it did me.

I wrap my arms around her, and she relaxes into me. "I'm not going anywhere, Soph. I promise. I won't lose you again."

The way she grips the back of my shirt makes my heart do things it hasn't done in years. It's odd but familiar—and something I'm determined to get used to again.

"Can I move in with you?"

The words shock my system.

What the hell is going on? First, Blaze started acting all weird, and then Dominic. And now the words that just dropped from Sophia's mouth are making me wonder if I'm hallucinating. Or in an alternate reality.

She just ran away from me. Now she wants to move in with me?

What game is she playing?

"Just for a little while?" She peeks up at me, her eyes wide. "It doesn't have to be super permanent."

"I—yes. Yes, of course. The more I have of you, the better." I kiss her gently, worried that if I use too much force she'll dissolve in my arms.

That solves that problem.

"Tonight?" She sniffles again.

"I wouldn't have it any other way. Why don't you start packing?"

She nods, but the rest of her body doesn't move. Her fingers are still fisting my shirt, and her breaths are uneven.

Tilting her chin up with a few fingers, I stare down into her perfectly blue eyes, still shining with unshed tears. "You're sure there's nothing else going on?"

She stares at me for a moment before whispering, "Positive." Then she finally lets go of me and heads into her room.

I watch her while she packs. She keeps tugging at the sleeves of her hoodie.

"I'll just take what I need for now." She pulls out a few sundresses from her closet, shoving them into her bag.

"Bring the yellow one."

Sophia pauses. "It was just one date, Xander. He's an asshole anyway."

Good.

Regardless, her words do nothing to soothe the jealousy that I've been wrestling with since I saw her in his arms. "Pack. the. dress."

She rolls her eyes and ignores me, opening a drawer and taking out some tiny shorts and tank tops. When she doesn't turn back to the closet, I step in front of her.

She lets out a small squeak, holding the pile of clothes to her chest.

"Don't test me, little bird."

Her eyes darken just a bit, the way they always do when I use her pet name. I take the opportunity and push her against the dresser.

Her mouth opens slightly when I snatch the clothes from her hands and throw them onto her bed. When my hand wraps lightly around her throat, she moans.

"I told you already, I'm not going to let you remember this dress as anything other than the one you wore while I fucked you until you screamed for the whole neighborhood to hear." I trace a finger down the front of her hoodie. "We can do that now, or we can do it later."

Her eyes widen. "Later. I'll pack the dress."

Satisfaction blooms in my chest. Stepping back, I watch as she snatches the dress from its hanger. Her cheeks are tinted pink.

I love seeing her flustered.

Once she's finished packing, I shoulder her bag. She's about to protest, but I raise my eyebrow at her.

She rolls her eyes, but her mouth stays shut.

The drive home is silent. I don't even have the radio on. The whole time, Sophia twirls a small ring around her finger.

By the time we pull into the garage, my patience is wearing thin. I'm tempted to drag her upstairs, tie her up, and deny her an orgasm until she tells me what's going on in that pretty little head of hers.

But I don't. Somehow, I manage to get all the way upstairs without so much as touching her.

"I'll clear out a few drawers and make some space in my closet." Setting her bag on the bed, I turn to face her.

Her eyes are still just a tad too wide, and she's still fiddling with her ring. "Thanks. And thanks for being so willing, Xander. I know it's short notice—"

I cut her off with a kiss that sends a shiver through her body.

To be honest, not having her here has been killing me. Not knowing what she's doing, wondering who she's with, who's making her smile and laugh.

It's been driving me mad.

"If I could, I'd never let you leave."

Then I step back, taking in the view.

Sophia. Here. In my bedroom—*our* bedroom. One day, I hope she fully recognizes the layout. It's been years, but it's still our house.

With a small smile, Sophia turns to unzip her bag. I stare at her for a few more seconds before getting to work rearranging my things. Thankfully, I have plenty of extra room in my closet. It just takes a minute of organizing things differently before Sophia has all the space she could need.

When I step back into my bedroom, Sophia has both her palms on my bed. She's leaning forward with her eyes closed.

"What's going on, Sophia?" There's no compassion in my voice, but I don't care. I'll wrench out all of her secrets until she's laying bare beneath me. I don't care how long it takes.

She jumps at my voice. "What's—what's going on?"

"You're hiding something. Don't you *dare* lie to me."

Shaking her head, she says, "I'm fine, Xander. I promise."

I'm on her in an instant, flipping her around and throwing her onto the bed. She squeals as she lands on her back.

Straddling her hips, I pin her arms beside her. "You can't hide things from me, so don't try."

"Xander," she gasps, squirming underneath me. "Please—please don't."

I lean down until I'm mere inches from her face. "Then come clean."

"Get off me," she whispers. Her voice is so small, so broken. What's even worse, there's fear in her eyes.

I don't hesitate. The second I'm off of her, she gasps in a breath, covering her face with her hands.

There are times when I can see it in her eyes that she wants me, even when she's glaring at me. But this—as I watch her curl up on top of my dark comforter, she looks so small. This is different than the times she eggs me on with her bad attitude.

A disgusting thought crosses my mind, and anger slashes through me. "Was it Brent? Did he do something to you?"

She shakes her head.

"You'd tell me if you were in danger, right? If you were in some sort of trouble."

"Of course, Xander." She sits up, wiping away a few tears. "Please just let this go."

Crossing my arms, I say, "I'll forget about it on one condition. You take the rest of the summer off from the coffee shop."

Her head snaps up. To my relief, she's glaring at me. "What?"

"Just for the summer. Work on your book. Stop killing yourself. I'll take care of you. And I'll keep paying your rent."

"You're fucking kidding me, right?"

I shake my head.

Truth is, I don't want to let her out of my sight. I practically shoved her into Tristan's path, and I'll do everything possible to keep her safe.

She's *mine*, and I'll protect her from anything and anyone who threatens her.

"That's ridiculous."

"No, what's ridiculous is that you're hiding something from me. This is your way out. Take it, or I'll wrench every single one of your secrets out of that pretty little head of yours."

Her nostrils flare, and her glare sharpens, but she stays silent. Finally, with a sigh, she says, "Fine."

I smirk, but I don't feel any satisfaction. Not when she's hiding something from me.

She scoops up her dresses and retreats to the closet. I can't help but stare after her.

Sophia may think she's off the hook, but it's only temporary.

Soon enough, I'll figure out what's bothering her.

And I'll make it fucking disappear.

CHAPTER 11

Sophia

The water stings my skin as I step down into the hot tub.

My wrists are still sensitive from the ropes Tristan left me in last night. Thankfully, though, they didn't bruise, and most of the redness has calmed since yesterday.

I scan the room, my gaze landing on the windows overlooking the dark lawn. Xander got a phone call just as we got down here, saying he'll join me in a few minutes.

I don't mind the time alone. The past twenty-four hours have been a disaster, and I need a fucking break.

First, Tristan. And then the threat that I could lose Xander.

After being with him yesterday, I just couldn't take it anymore. I called off from work so I could stay home and cry all day.

So, of course, Xander had to show up in the middle of one of my sobbing sessions. I told him it was because of a bad dream—*the* bad dream, and he seemed to believe me.

Until I couldn't shake off the fear that Xander has entered my life just to leave again. Between that and the thought that Tristan could break into my house anytime he pleases, I've been a mess.

Thankfully, Xander was more than happy to move me in with him. Ever since I saw him standing on my porch today, my body has been slowly relaxing. My chest doesn't feel like there's a hundred-pound weight on it anymore.

The sinking dread I felt last night hasn't left me. Neither have the sharp stabs of fear any time Xander forces himself on top of me.

But I'm safe—safer, anyway.

As I sink onto the seat that wraps around the tub, I let out a loud sigh. I've got to figure out a plan.

First, stop acting all skittish around Xander before he takes back our deal. I'm too afraid of what Tristan will do if I don't follow his instructions.

Second, figure out what Tristan has on Xander—without anyone finding out. I'm not terribly confident about my abilities to do that, but I have to try.

Third, find some way to stop Tristan. There's something bigger going on here. And if Dominic's and Alexander's argument from the other night means anything, it's that they're involved.

So how do I tip them off that Tristan has the power to take Xander away? Do they already know?

I hear the door slam shut, followed by heavy footsteps.

"That was Dominic. We have some . . . stuff we have to take care of. He's on his way over along with Blaze and Felix." He takes his shirt off in a smooth motion before joining me. "I have a few minutes."

I smile as relief floods me. Having Blaze around will probably put me more at ease. But I can't wait—I need to get back to acting normal. Now.

When Alexander settles next to me, I drape my legs over his and place my hand on his chest. He raises an eyebrow at me.

"I'm sorry about earlier. I think I'm just PMS-ing."

He lets out a low hum before dropping a kiss on my lips. It's short, but it still shoots electricity through my veins. "Just as long as I can touch you."

I gasp as he lifts my chin with a finger and kisses my neck slowly. He pulls me onto his lap, cradling me as his lips move lower, lower . . .

"Xander!"

He slips my bikini's straps off my shoulders, letting my breasts fall free. With a groan, he takes one of my nipples into his mouth. I can't help the sound that leaves my lips.

As he palms my ass, his free hand squeezes my other breast. I let my head fall back, my hair dipping into the water.

"How much time do we have?"

"Enough to make you come from one finger and my mouth."

Keeping his mouth on my breast, he slides a hand in between my legs. He shoves my bikini bottoms to the side and begins to circle my clit.

In this moment, I'm wholly his. I don't need Tristan's threats to keep me close to him. And I'll do anything to make sure we both stay together.

Xander sucks on my nipple, quickening his finger. I moan. My nails dig into his muscular shoulders as I fight the urge to grind against him. His touch has a way of taking over my whole body. It's like the second his hands are on me, I'm no longer in control—he is.

And as the water from the tub mixes with the slickness of my arousal, adding in just the right amount of friction, I wouldn't have it any other way.

Giving Xander control of my body is like flying, like soaring above the treetops and riding the wind. In his arms, I'm the freest I've ever been.

When I come, it's with a loud moan. My hips buck against his hand. It's only when he removes his hand that I shudder and collapse against his chest.

"You're so fucking hot," he groans.

We hear voices echoing in the hallway, and my post-orgasm bliss is cut short. Quickly, I pull up the straps of my bikini and spring off of Alexander. When the guys filter into the room, the only indication that Alexander just wrecked me completely is my heaving chest.

"Fuck, Alex, why didn't you tell us to bring our trunks?" Blaze grins, winking at me.

"Mixing business with pleasure only leads to disaster," Dominic says, shooting his brother a look. Blaze flips him off.

I can't help but smile. Dominic has always been serious. While it can be annoying, right now it's comforting. Familiar.

"Well, are we meeting in here?" Felix glances around before his eyes stop on the view out the tall windows.

"What's this about?" I stand, running my fingers through my hair.

The guys all hesitate, their gazes landing on Xander. Dominic is giving him an accusing glare.

Tristan. This must be about Tristan.

The urge to come clean hits me like a tidal wave. These three were my backup, my safety net. They never let anything happen to me in high school. I can trust them.

My eyes slide to Felix. He may be related to the Graysons, but I don't know him. What if he's secretly working for Tristan? What if, somehow, Tristan has Xander's whole house bugged?

I have eyes everywhere.

Gulping, I clench my fists underwater. The idea of finding safety in telling the guys about Tristan's blackmailing is tempting. But the thought of Tristan ripping Xander away from me is terrifying. I can't bear the thought of losing him—even if he's turned into a mystery.

"Don't worry about it." Xander kisses the top of my head before heading out of the hot tub. "We won't take too long. Feel free to stay in here, or hang out wherever you'd like. I asked Anna to set out some snacks in the kitchen. What's mine is yours."

I stare at him a second too long.

What's mine is yours.

"You good, Soph?" Blaze's voice is amused.

"Great," I say. I can't take my eyes off of Alexander, and he meets my gaze with a cool, calm stare.

How can he keep his composure when he says stuff like that? And how can he be so willing to take care of me? He's even offered to pay my rent. Which, to be honest, I see as a huge red flag.

I learned from watching my mother that being financially dependent on a man can ruin you. But what am I supposed to do? Tristan wants me to get close to Xander. Moving in with him—while making sure he doesn't try to force out my secret—seems like the best move.

And that means holding up my end of the deal. No more income.

The guys leave, and I only stay in the hot tub for a few more minutes. I may have to quit the coffee shop, but I still have my book. And this is some prime writing time.

So I dry off and head back to the bedroom.

Maybe I'll be able to distract myself from the mess my life has become.

Upstairs, I get changed and grab my laptop. Xander has a sitting room off of his bedroom that I haven't seen him use much. With a smile, I settle onto a dark green couch in front of an empty fireplace. I swear, it's like he has a little apartment inside this house.

Just like—

No.

Oh god.

How have I not put together the pieces until now?

The bathroom, with the giant tub and the big window, just like we always planned it. A sitting room off of our bedroom so I'd have a place to escape when his family stayed with us.

A writing room for me on the first floor, with French doors and lots of windows looking out into a forest.

Letting out a breath, I turn back to the bedroom. Where had we decided to put the writing room? In the back of the house, of course. Close to the kitchen?

Without it even registering in my head, my feet take me back downstairs. The floors are cold against my bare feet, but I hardly feel it.

We'd designed many houses together in our spare time, but there was one that was our favorite. And now, walking through the hallways, I can't believe I didn't see it before.

How could I forget?

Passing through the kitchen, I notice that the cabinets are painted black, just like Xander likes, and the countertops are white marble—just how I always said I wanted them.

A few rooms down, I find a pair of French doors painted white. With only a moment's hesitation, I push them open.

Once I flip the light on, I gasp. A small chandelier hangs over a desk in the middle of the room. Large windows look out over the yard and the dark forest. A small, red couch sits in a small corner, just like I always wanted.

It's . . . *perfect.*

And he did this for me. For us.

With a breath, I remember his words the first time he brought me here.

I want to see you in my house.

"Xander," I call out, turning back down the hall.

Where is he meeting with the guys? His office?

Making my way across the house, I call for him again. And again, once I'm closer.

"Soph?" I hear his voice drifting through the dark hallway, tense with alarm. "What's wrong?"

"Xan," I gasp, running in the direction of his voice until I spot him, stalking toward me.

Once I'm close, I jump into his arms, wrapping my legs around his waist and clutching his shoulders. With a half-sob, half-laugh, I bury my face into the crook of his neck.

"What's going on?" He holds me tightly, protectively. "Are you all right?"

"I'm perfect," I say, pulling away and cradling his face in my hands. "God, Xan. You're crazy."

He just looks at me, his brows furrowed. In the dim lighting of the hallway, I can barely see the gold flecks in his eyes. But they're there, becoming more apparent as his expression softens. "You found your writing room, didn't you?"

"You built our house," I whisper. "For me."

With a light kiss on my jawbone, he says, "For us, little bird. I told you—I've never stopped loving you. And I never will."

I open my mouth to repeat those words back to him, but I stop myself.

Not yet. Not with Tristan's threat looming over us. Soon, once I know Xander will be safe, I'll say those words completely on my own. *Without it being what Tristan wants.*

So instead, I kiss him. It's the only way I can express the swell in my heart and the butterflies in my stomach. If I didn't have enough proof that Alexander's actions were sincere, this would've been it.

He's *mine*, forever. *Forever.*

With a grunt, Xander presses my back into the wall. Our kiss is an explosion of lips and tongue and teeth, anything but soft and gentle.

"I've been waiting for you to notice," he says, palming my ass. "You're fucking *everywhere* in this house. Living without you here, but with everything reminding me of you—Christ. I'm never letting you leave."

"You're the one who did that to yourself," I say, giggling. "You didn't have to build *this* house."

One of his hands leaves my ass, only for it to be replaced by a loud *smack* and a stinging sensation. I gasp, wincing slightly at the pain, but I can't deny the butterflies leaving my stomach and going somewhere *else*.

"Watch that pretty little mouth of yours, little bird."

Someone down the hall clears their throat, and we turn to find Dominic glaring at us, arms crossed. "We still have things to discuss, Alex."

Grateful for the darkness hiding the blush creeping up my cheeks, I give Xander a peck on the cheek before squirming out of his arms.

When he disappears into his office, I take a deep breath. Then I wander back through the house—*our* house. To *our* bedroom.

. . .

After their meeting, the guys hang around for a movie. Brooke shows up with beer and a forced smile. She sits next to me on the couch, where Xander has me cozily tucked into his side.

Squeezing her hand, I give her what I hope is a warm smile. When I let go, I notice her hands are shaking.

"You good?" I whisper as the movie starts.

She just nods, settling in and sipping her beer.

I turn back to the TV, just to notice Blaze watching us. His expression is unreadable, but the way he's gripping his beer makes me wonder if there's something going on between the two of them.

They'd make one hell of a cute couple. Blaze is tall and broad-shouldered, and while Brooke is by no means frail, she's tiny. And they're both ridiculously attractive.

I tuck the thought away. I'll have to pester Blaze about who his latest crush is later. For now, I burrow deeper into Xander's hold. His arm tightens around me, and I smile at the warmth spreading through me.

The movie starts, and I can't help the wave of nostalgia that washes over me. It's just like old times—a movie, my closest friends all in one room, and Xander's arm wrapped around me.

I've missed this so much.

About fifteen minutes into the movie, Brooke's phone starts going off. She freezes when she sees the name flashing across the screen.

David.

Before anyone else sees, she angles the phone toward herself and gets up, excusing herself. I watch her go, noting the tension in her steps.

Brooke is the sweetest person I've ever known. It kills me to see her so miserable.

And that's why I get up, telling Xander I have to pee. I don't know who David is, but based on her reaction, I'd bet a lot of money he's one of her exes.

I enter the hallway quietly, noticing that one of the French doors that leads outside is slightly ajar. Slowly, I open it more and slip through it.

Brooke is standing a few feet away, facing into the dark night. The voice on the other end is so loud, I can hear it.

"I know you stole that hard drive," a male voice shouts.

"You shouldn't've left it at my house. Did you think I wouldn't find it? I'm not stupid, David." Her voice is surprisingly strong.

"I need it back, you bitch. Tonight."

Brooke snorts. "I don't owe you anything."

"You don't want to know what I'm capable of. Bring it by the bar. You have a half hour."

"Oh, I know *exactly* what you're capable of. Go fuck yourself." Brooke spits the words out and then hangs up.

I disappear back inside and hide in the bathroom before she sees me. Once I hear her shut the door, I wait another minute before returning to the living room.

When I settle back down next to Xander, I give Brooke a small glance. She's sitting rigidly, with her knees tucked under her chin. She looks so small all folded up like that. It reminds me of the girl who used to hide in her closet whenever her parents fought.

Xander's lips on my neck bring my attention back to him. "You good?" he murmurs in my ear. "You're tense."

"I'm fine." I bite my lip. Should I tell him about Brooke's phone call? I don't want to overstep, but that guy sounded pissed.

No. Brooke's life is hers. I already spied on her. I'm not going to betray her trust even more by telling Xander something she seems to want to keep private.

So I snuggle into his side and watch the movie. One of Xander's hands slips under my shirt. His fingers graze my stomach and send shivers through me.

"Not here," I hiss, elbowing him.

"I'm ready to kidnap you upstairs," he whispers. "All I've been able to think of since earlier is you. The way you sounded when you came had me rock hard, little bird. And then the way you ran to me, and kissed me? You can't expect me to *not* need to be inside of you."

Want stirs in my stomach, but I shake my head. "Absolutely not. I'd be so embarrassed."

He groans quietly, biting the shell of my ear. "I can think of nothing better than dragging you away so they all know that you're mine. For good."

I squirm at the heat gathering between my legs. Then I whisper, "No," before turning back to the TV. This isn't the time.

We watch the rest of the movie without incident. Xander's hands don't leave my body, but he doesn't push me into anything I'm uncomfortable with. I've always loved that about him.

As soon as the credits start rolling, Brooke shoots up out of her seat. "I'm gonna get going. I have an early morning tomorrow."

We hug, and then Brooke kisses Xander on the cheek.

"What?! Where's my kiss?" Felix blocks her way, grinning like a little kid.

With a giggle, Brooke stands on her tiptoes and pecks his cheek. He holds her in place for a moment, murmuring something in her ear, but she shakes her head. Blaze glares daggers at Felix behind her back, who smirks.

"I'll walk you out." Blaze stands from his chair and straightens his shirt.

"I'll be fine." Brooke gives him a thin smile before turning to go. "Have a good night, everyone."

"You too," Dominic says. He turns to Xander, and they have some sort of silent conversation before moving to the far side of the room and speaking in hushed tones.

Once Brooke is gone, Felix lets out a snicker. "You've got it bad, dude."

"I'm gonna kill you," Blaze growls.

But Felix is barely paying attention to him. Instead, he's heading straight toward me. "Sophia, do you know who Brooke was on the phone with?"

"What? Uh, no. I was in the bathroom."

He raises an eyebrow, unamused. "I know you were listening."

I bite my lip. This isn't any of Felix's business. Hell, it's not even mine.

"Did you not see how tense she was?" Blaze snaps. His voice is slightly raised, and I get the feeling he can't control it. "She sat there on the couch like a cornered little kid."

"It could be nothing, Blaze. Maybe she had a bad day. So just chill. David doesn't even know she's found the hard drive yet."

I tense. That's *exactly* what Brooke's phone call had been about. "Who's David?"

"Her ex-fiancé," Felix says, flopping into an overstuffed chair. "The fucker is—"

"That's enough." Xander rejoins our conversation, pulling me into him. When he looks down at me, his brows furrow. "What's wrong?"

I hesitate. But looking around the room, I find three men with nothing but concern in their eyes. Concern for Brooke. Whatever just happened, the only thing they care about is Brooke's safety.

"If she *was* on the phone with David," I say slowly, "then that would be a bad thing?"

Felix's face falls, and he leans forward. "Very. He's dangerous. Was it him?"

I nod.

"What did he want?" Xander's voice is completely calm. When I hesitate, he strokes my arm. "I need the absolute truth from you, Sophia."

"He—he asked her about a hard drive. Said he wanted it back. Then he threatened her."

Blaze swears, grabbing his keys from the coffee table. "I'm going over there. If anything happens to her—goddammit, I knew she shouldn't've moved back out on her own."

Dominic moves to stop him, but Xander holds up a hand.

"Out of all of you, he has her best interest at heart the most. And I'm not leaving Sophia's side unless I have to."

Dominic grits his teeth but nods. Blaze is already rushing out the door, yelling that he'll text with updates when he has them.

"What exactly did David say?" Dominic snaps, whirling to face me. "Verbatim."

"He just said that she didn't know what he was capable of. Then he told her to bring the hard drive to the bar, and that she had half an hour. But that was . . ." I trail off, glancing at my phone for the time. "Almost two hours ago."

Leaning forward in his seat, Felix says, "Dom, do you want me to go after him? Just in case things get messy."

Messy? What kind of messy? What the hell is going on?

Dominic shakes his head. "Blaze can handle himself. Just make sure the drive is secure." With that, he starts pacing the length of the living room. "I hoped we'd have more time."

I glance between the three men. Worry is etched into their faces, although I can barely tell when I look at Xander. Hell, I might even be projecting.

But that's not what matters. Their mysterious meeting earlier already had my curiosity piqued. And now this? If they have David's hard drive, does that mean it's connected to whatever shit they've got going on with Tristan? Does that mean Brooke is involved?

A shiver runs through me, and I couldn't be more grateful when Xander pulls me into him. My head rests on his chest, and I take in his perfect smell.

"What's going on?" I say, wrapping an arm around Xander's waist.

I'm met with silence.

"Okay, seriously?" Pulling away from Xander, I glare at all three of them. "Is Brooke in trouble? And why the fuck don't you want to protect your sister?" I poke Xander in the chest.

"Because he wants to protect *you*." Dominic steps forward with his hands shoved into his pockets. His eyes are dark, brooding. "Which he'd be able to do if he'd tell you the goddamn truth."

"She's already too involved as it is," Xander says. "The less she knows, the better."

"That's not your call to make." Dominic is standing in front of us, his glare directed over my head at the man holding me.

Squirming away from Xander, I say, "He's right. It's mine. Tell me what the fuck is going on."

But Xander stays silent, and when I turn to Dominic, his lips are pressed together in a thin line. He won't even look at me—it's like he's in some sort of staring contest with Xan.

Typical. The three of them have always shared an undying loyalty toward each other. Even now, when Dom so obviously thinks Xander is in the wrong, he's keeping his mouth shut.

With a yell of frustration, I throw my hands up in the air. These men are ridiculous. "I'm going to bed. Text me when you hear from Blaze."

Xander catches my arm before I've even taken two steps. He pulls me against his chest, capturing my lips in a kiss. "I'll join you soon."

I head deeper into the house, taking the stairs two-by-two.

Only once I'm in our bedroom do I glance at my phone. What I see makes my stomach drop.

Unknown Number: Go through Alexander's things. I need to know what he has on me. You have until midnight.

Of course. How could I expect this to be easy? If Tristan has a person on the inside, there's no way he's going to pass up the opportunity to get some snooping done. Heading back the way I came, I stop in front of Xander's office. Right now, he's distracted by the guys. This might be my only chance to sneak around.

Reaching out, I turn the knob, but it barely moves. Locked.

I enter the next room—a massive library, complete with a balcony overlooking the pool area. And if I'm lucky . . .

Stepping outside, I peer to my left. Yes! There's a door farther down that has to lead into the office, along with a window or two.

Of course, the door is locked. But one of the windows is slightly open, probably to let in a breeze. I pry out the screen and shove it up before climbing inside.

It's dark, but I don't dare turn a light on. Instead, I use the flashlight on my phone. The computer is password-protected, and most of the drawers of his desk are locked. But two aren't.

Without hesitation, I open the first. There's a stack of papers, but it all has to do with insurance. I find a small, black flash drive and stuff it into my pocket. I'll plug it into my laptop later.

I pull open the second drawer and freeze. There, sitting on top of a notebook, is a gun. The metal glints in the moonlight.

A gun. Why would Xander need a gun? He has plenty of security. And who'd want to hurt him anyway?

Tristan.

"Don't touch that."

I yelp. Whirling around, I find a large figure standing in front of the window I entered from. My knees give out, even as I realize it's Xander, and I grab onto the edge of the desk. "What—I—how—Xander, I can—" I stop. Explain? How?

He steps toward me, lifting me so I'm sitting on the desk. With one arm around me, he uses the other to softly close the drawer. When the gun disappears from sight, I let out a small breath of relief.

"I get an alert whenever an outside door or window opens. Nice thinking, taking the balcony to get in here. And thanks for reminding me I left the window open."

I shiver. He forgot to close it? That means anyone could've climbed up to the balcony and gotten in. Tristan could've gotten in and found me. Tied me up again.

Xan would never let that happen.

"Soph?" Xander brushes his fingers across my cheek.

"W-what?"

"The flash drive."

I look down. He's opened the top drawer, revealing the insurance papers and the missing flash drive I pocketed. With a breath of disappointment, I fish it out and place it in his palm.

Once the drawer is closed, he sighs. "I meant it when I said what's mine is yours, Soph. But the things in here don't concern you."

"Actually, I'm quite concerned." I glance up at him. He's perfectly calm, without even a hint of annoyance showing. "What's going on with Brooke and this David guy?"

"It doesn't concern you."

"That's not your call," I snap, pushing against his chest. "Do I need to drag Dominic into this?"

Xander chuckles. "Dominic is on my side, little bird. He knows I'll kill him if he interferes with your safety."

"My safety."

He runs a hand through my hair before placing a kiss on my forehead. "I know you're curious. But you don't need to know."

"Xan. Am I in danger?" Dominic's words echo through my mind.

You're fucking with her life.

"Not if you trust me. I trust you, sweetheart. Can you do the same?"

My words catch in my throat. He trusts me. *He trusts me.*

Even if Tristan hadn't barged into my room, I still would've said yes to Xander. I want this to work out. But now? Now I'm here, in Xander's house, practically Tristan's puppet.

And he *trusts* me.

Shoving down the self-loathing creeping through my chest, I look up and into Xander's perfectly brown eyes. "I'm trying to."

"Then take a leap of faith." He leans down, and his lips graze my neck. "I promise I wouldn't do anything to hurt you."

Under different circumstances, maybe I would've let it go. But now? I have to find out a way to get out from under Tristan's thumb. But in the meantime, I need information.

"If I'm not allowed to keep secrets from you, then why are you allowed to keep secrets from me?" I say.

Xander raises an eyebrow. He lifts my chin with two fingers, forcing me to keep eye contact with him. "You *are* keeping a secret from me, little bird. Or are you planning on coming clean?"

My breath hitches as he traces a finger up my stomach and in between my breasts, stopping at the base of my throat. I shake my head.

"Then let it go." His voice is low, and he's so close I can smell the alcohol on his breath. "And don't ever go behind my back like this again."

"I won't," I whisper.

He leans down to kiss me, but just then, his phone goes off. In an instant, he yanks his phone out of his pocket. "Blaze. How's my sister?" He pauses. "Is she all right?"

He grunts in frustration before pulling his phone away and dialing a different number. He waits impatiently, tapping a finger against my arm. "Yes, Doctor Shepherd. Brooke's been attacked. I need you to go to her place and check her out." He listens for a moment before saying, "Possible concussion. She stayed conscious, though." After a quick exchange of Brooke's address, he hangs up.

"Is she okay?" I wrap my arms around his waist, peering up at him.

"She'll be fine. Now, come with me." He takes my hand in his, pulling me off the desk and out of the office. Then down a hallway or two until we're in his bedroom.

"Xan, I'm not tired."

He turns to face me then, his expression hard. "You're going to bed. And you're not leaving this room until tomorrow morning."

"Xander!"

Picking me up, he throws me onto the bed. "I have some things to deal with, and I need to know you're safe—and not getting into more trouble in my office."

"This is ridiculous."

He's silent for a moment before leaning over me. "My sister could've died tonight. I'll be damned if I involve you too, Sophia. I'm *not* losing you. So you can stay here, where I know you'll be safe, or I'll tie you up so you can't leave. Which will it be?"

My breath catches as he pins my arms to the bed. I know he didn't mean it in *that* way, but want still floods my body. "Xan . . ."

"I need you to stay put." His voice turns uneven, just for a moment, and I see something I've never seen before—Alexander Hendricks, afraid.

My heart squeezes, and I nod. "I'll stay. I promise."

With a sigh, he closes his eyes and rests his forehead against mine. "Thank you." Then, with a light kiss, he leaves.

And I stay. I stay, even though the world feels like it's crashing down on me. Because that look on his face—god, that *look*.

I can't go behind his back. I can't break my promise to him.

So instead, I text Tristan, begging for more time.

And as I burrow underneath the dark comforter, taking deep breaths to calm my pattering heart, I realize what I have to do.

Take a leap of faith.

Chapter 12

Alexander

"How is she?" I take a sip of the coffee Dominic brought me. Last night, he went to Brooke's to help secure the house. Apparently, my little sister didn't want Blaze to leave her side. Which is fine by me—I already called and told him he's not allowed to let Brooke out of his sight.

"Better, I think. When I stopped over this morning, she said she was just sore and dealing with a killer headache."

"Good." Brooke is small, but she's strong. She's always been able to handle whatever life throws at her.

For the most part, that is.

We're in the kitchen as the sun rises over the treetops. I gave Anna the morning off, since I'm not sure when Sophia is going to wake up. She tossed and turned all night, so I'm letting her sleep as much as she needs.

"We have a problem on our hands, though."

My eyes snap up to meet Dominic's. He looks even more grim than usual. "What?"

"She told him we have the drive."

"Fuck."

Up until now, we've been able to track Tristan's movements without his knowledge—or at least without him getting too suspicious. We've stayed under the radar, learning as much as we possible can. When we realized David might be involved, things got complicated. Even more so when, a few days ago, Brooke found a hard drive he'd stashed in her house.

Stupid move on his part.

Of course, Tristan probably already had suspicions that we were onto him. We did try going to the authorities when we put the pieces together on a few of his most recent kills. When that didn't work, we had to resort to other methods—taking him down ourselves.

But now? Not only does Tristan have rock-solid proof that we're on his case, but he also has a decade-old hate for me. The feeling is mutual.

"We need to up our game."

Dominic nods in agreement. "And we need to be careful. Tristan is a trained killer, and so are his men. We're good at what we do, but we aren't perfect. Keep Sophia close. Do you want a detail on your mother?"

I rub my face. My mother is more of a nuisance to me than anything else, but she's still my mother. And Brooke would be devastated if anything happened to her. "Just keep an eye on her. She doesn't need to know anything's up."

With a curt nod, Dom turns to go. But he pauses. "Look, I know it's none of my business. But Sophia—"

"You're right. None of your business."

He whips back around at my harsh tone. "I care about her too, Alex. And the less you tell her, the more she'll look for answers on her own."

He's right and we both know it. She already tried. But I don't care. The less she knows, the less likely she is to get scared off. I need her close right now.

"Alex, just tell her something. Anything to keep her at bay."

"I'll think of something."

Dominic shakes his head and leaves, slamming the door behind him.

I drain the rest of my coffee. I've got to get to work, but there's something I need to do first.

Upstairs, I find my bed empty. The bathroom door opens, and Sophia slips through, only half-dressed in leggings and a bra.

"Good morning," I say, and she jumps.

"Oh—Xander. I woke up and you were gone. I overslept."

"You needed it." I'm in front of her in a few steps, pulling her into my chest and planting a kiss on the top of her head. "Do you feel rested?"

She shrugs, pulling away. "Xander, about last night—I'm sorry for breaking into your office. I'm just scared, and I want to know—"

I press a finger to her soft lips. "Not now. Later." Leaning down, I kiss her gently until she moans. When I feel her arms encircle my neck, I lift her up until her legs are wrapped around me, too.

"Xander," she whispers before I capture her lips in another kiss.

Years ago, I wondered if I'd ever be able to get enough of Sophia. Now that I have her back, older and even more beautiful, I know I never will. The way she feels against me, the way she moans softly whenever I touch her—it'll never become less addictive.

Sophia's kisses slow to a stop, and she rests her head on my shoulder. "I missed you this morning."

"I had some things I had to deal with. I promise it won't become a habit." It won't. Waking up with Sophia next to me is a bliss I thought I'd lost forever. I'll never stop cherishing it.

Her stomach growls, and I smile. "Dominic dropped off coffee and donuts. They're in the kitchen."

She moans, nestling her face into the crook of my neck. Holding her close, I carry her downstairs. When I set her on the counter, she lets go reluctantly.

I watch her as she nibbles on a donut, taking sips of coffee in between. Her blonde hair is in a loose ponytail, and the morning sun catches it perfectly, giving it a soft glow.

She smiles up at me. "Do you have an update on Brooke?"

"She got a little beat up, but other than a minor concussion, she's fine."

"Do you want to see her?"

"No, we'll see her at my mother's birthday party tomorrow. Ah, fuck. I meant to tell you about it earlier this week."

Sophia grimaces. "I don't think Everly will appreciate me showing up to her party. And since when do you forget things? You have a scarily-good memory."

I pull her coffee cup from her hands and set it on the counter. Cupping her cheeks, I lean my forehead against hers. "I have no need to remember things I don't care about."

She bites her lip. Her blue eyes are shining up at me, innocent and hopeful. She doesn't say anything—doesn't tell me that I should care about my mother. Doesn't tell me that I'm an awful son. Instead, she just nods.

"God, I love you." I kiss her, tasting the sweetness from the donut and the bitterness from the coffee. She moans, and I bite her bottom lip.

When she opens her legs, I grab her thighs and pull her to the edge of the counter. She gasps, grabbing onto my arms.

"I won't let you fall," I murmur against her lips. She whimpers as I yank her leggings and panties down in one go.

This. This is what I've been craving for the past twenty-four hours.

She unclasps her bra, revealing her milky white breasts. Her nipples are rosy and hardened, begging for my tongue.

With one hand holding her, I dip her backward and take one into my mouth. Her high-pitched moan sends a zap of pleasure through me.

I undo my pants and shove them down. "Do you want me, little bird?"

"Yes," she says, her voice breathy and light. Her legs wrap around my waist. "Please, Xan."

I position myself at her entrance and slide in an inch or two. "Fuck, you're already soaked."

We both moan as I roll my hips forward and fill her. My thumb circles her clit, and her head tilts back. When I pick up my pace, she digs her nails into my arms. I groan at the pain, slamming into her.

I want this to last forever, but it has to be quick. So I angle my hips to hit one of her sweet spots, stroking her clit with my finger.

"Xan," she moans. Her whole body tenses. "Oh fuck, oh god. Xander!" She screams as she arches her back, and I come with her.

I lighten the touch of my finger on her clit, still stroking softly. This woman—*this woman.* She couldn't be any more perfect.

She holds onto my shoulders, looking into my eyes. Her lips are slightly swollen from kissing me, and her face is slack from her post-orgasm haze.

Beautiful. Absolutely perfect.

And completely *mine.*

. . .

I spend the whole day locked in my office, only coming out to check on Sophia and to eat.

As the day passes, she becomes increasingly restless. Sure, she's been able to write all day, but the secrets between us are getting to her. But I can't tell her—I just can't. The less she knows, the better off she is.

So I get to work, making phone call after phone call, plotting away.

By the end of the day, we have half a plan:

Apparently Felix has a way to get to David's maid, which gives us someone on the inside. And Dominic says he might have a lead, but the fucker is being all mysterious about it.

And Blaze is working on coordinating a group of guys from Grayson Security to tail Tristan and David. We've tried before, but they've always caught on. So we need to find ways to follow them more conspicuously.

Once we can find where they're operating from, we can finally take them down—for good.

The thought of killing should scare me, or make me feel some kind of guilt. I shouldn't *want* to kill anyone. But I promised myself a long time ago that I'd do whatever is necessary to keep what's mine safe. And I've kept that promise, dammit. I'm not going back now.

There's a soft knock on the door, and I jerk up. How long have I been staring out the window?

"Come in," I say, running a hand through my hair.

Sophia pops her head in with a timid smile. "Hey. I just wanted to see if you were hungry."

For a moment, I just stare at her. She's in shorts and a tank top, with her hair in a messy bun. Completely relaxed, like she's made a decision that's been weighing on her for some time. I'll never get enough of seeing her walking around my home.

"Xan?"

I glance at my phone. It's already after six, and I have a text from Anna saying she has dinner ready. "Yeah, let's eat."

Sophia's smile widens as I step toward her and take her into my arms. Her frame molds perfectly into mine, like we were made for each other.

"I'm sorry I've been in here all day," I murmur. "Some things came up."

"Like some things with David?" She peeks up at me.

I nod.

"What was on the hard drive, Xan? I can't imagine he'd attack Brooke over personal stuff."

"Personal stuff?"

"Yeah. You know, like sex tapes. If Brooke is into that kind of thing. Or maybe David filmed them without her permission."

"I have no desire to think about my sister's sex life."

"So it isn't something personal."

"Sophia," I say, her name a warning on my lips. But her gaze hardens.

"Just tell me something. Anything, Xan."

Tracing my fingers up and down her spine, I sigh. Dominic is right—I need to tell her something so she doesn't try to break into my office again. Or worse. "I can't tell you much. Just stay away from Tristan tomorrow, okay? He's dangerous."

Her eyes widen, and I feel her entire body shudder. "Tristan? He's involved with whatever's going on with David and Brooke?"

"That's all you're getting out of me, little bird. Unless you're willing to come clean." It's not the truth, but the lie comes out smoothly. Regardless of whether Sophia comes clean or not, I can't tell her the whole truth.

As far as I'm concerned, she'll never know what I've done.

Her gaze falls to my chest, and her shoulders droop. She's trying to hide it—the fear—but I can still see it behind her eyes. "Let's just eat," she mumbles.

Taking her hand in mine, I lead her down to the kitchen. Anna has food set out on the counter for us, and I give her a thankful smile.

After sitting on one of the island stools, Sophia barely even picks at her food. Her leg is bouncing under the counter as she takes a sip of water. "Do you have more work to do today?" she asks.

"I'm all yours."

"I want to go on a walk with you. In the woods."

Interesting. Sophia never was much of a nature person. I suppose there are lots of ways a person can change in five years.

"All right," I say. "We'll go on a walk as soon as we're done eating."

Chapter 13

Sophia

I grip Xander's hand as we head up a path surrounded by trees. The leaves shelter us from the sun, but it's still warm.

"You don't have security cameras out here, right?" I turn to face him.

He chuckles. "Are you planning on doing something you don't want caught on camera?"

My cheeks heat, but I roll my eyes. "Answer the question."

"No security cameras." Pulling me in close, he brushes a few strands of my hair out of my face. "It's just you and me, little bird."

His touch sends tendrils of electricity through me, but I step back. Not now.

I've been thinking all day that whatever is going on with Brooke has to be connected to Tristan blackmailing me. It just couldn't be a coincidence. So when Xander confirmed it earlier, any doubts I had about coming clean left me.

For some reason, Xander and the Graysons are in some type of war against Tristan and David. I don't know the details, but I do know one thing: the more information they have, the better.

Then take a leap of faith.

"I'm going to tell you everything."

Xander stills. His face falls blank, turning neutral and unreadable. "Go on," he says slowly.

I glance around one last time. "You're sure we're alone?"

"Yes, of course." Reaching out, Xander takes hold of my arm. "Soph, what's wrong?"

"Tristan is blackmailing me," I blurt. My hands are beginning to shake.

Xander's features harden, and his hand tightens around my arm. "*What?*"

"I'm so sorry, Xan. I wanted to tell you—I promise. But he told me that—he told me—" My voice breaks, and I cover my face with my hands. I'd been hoping to avoid getting emotional, but all the fear I've been bottling up is ready to explode inside me.

"Explain. Now." His voice is harsh, and I cringe.

"He—he broke into my house the night before you took me to the diner. He said that he had something on you, that he had the power to destroy you, to take you away from me."

Xander's hand falls from my arm, and even though it's summer, coldness seeps into my skin. "Then what?"

Wringing my hands, I say, "He told me to get close to you. He said he wanted to break you, and destroy you. And that if I told you, he'd have you arrested. Xander, what did you do?"

He stares at me for a moment. The softness that's usually there for me is gone. "That's why you broke into my office last night."

"Xan, I'm sorry. I didn't want—"

"Is that why you wanted to move in with me?" he snaps. He grabs my shoulders and slams my back into a tree. "Is that why?"

"No! Not entirely. I knew it'd keep him at bay for a while, but mostly I was scared. I thought he might break in again, and tie—" I cut myself off, my eyes widening. I don't want to tell him this part. It's slightly embarrassing that Tristan managed to tie me up while I was sleeping, and I didn't wake up even a bit.

My heart beats wildly as he stares at me with hard eyes. It hadn't occurred to me that Xander might not believe me, might not trust me after this.

Of course that's how he feels. You betrayed him.

"He tied you up."

I stare at the ground, clenching my fists to stop them from shaking. "Xander, I—"

"What else did he do?"

My eyes squeeze shut as tears form in my eyes. I have no desire to relive that night.

"What. else. did. he. do." Xander presses me further into the tree, leaning forward until I can feel his breath on my face. His voice is lethal.

"He kissed me," I whisper. "And hit me." Tears fall onto my cheeks. When I move to wipe them away, Xander catches my wrist in his hand.

"Why the *fuck* didn't you tell me?" His voice is full of disgust, of hate.

I sniffle, still avoiding his glare. This was a mistake—I should've done what Tristan said and kept my mouth shut. Now I'm going to lose Xander. He's never going to trust me again, and what we've managed to rekindle will go up in flames.

"Sophia," he snaps, grabbing my chin and turning it to face him. His eyes are cold, full of fury.

"He said he'd take you away," I whisper. "He said he knows everything. Xander, he knew we were meeting the next day. He knew what we were going to be talking about. I don't know how, but he did."

He stays silent, but his grip on me doesn't loosen.

"Xan, what does he have on you?"

"That doesn't concern you."

Fair enough.

"You wouldn't tell me this in the house. Did he bug it? Did you?"

"I didn't, I swear. I don't know if he did. He just said that he knows everything. That he has eyes everywhere."

Taking a deep breath, Xander finally steps back. And somehow, the absence of his touch is worse than him pinning me to the tree.

"Xander," I beg, "I need you to understand. I'd already decided what I wanted before Tristan broke in. I'd already made up my mind—I want you, Xan. I wish I would've told you, but I was scared. I don't know what he has on you, but it sounds serious. Please, Xan—"

"Shut up." His words are curt, and he won't even look at me.

I cover my mouth to stifle my sobs, but it barely does anything.

Oh god, he can't stand me. He hates me.

Xander begins pacing, his hands locked behind his back. My feet stay frozen to the ground, and even if I wanted to move, I don't think I could.

I don't know how much time passes. I just watch as Xander stalks back and forth on the path, the sunlight casting odd patterns on his body. Even though I'm pretty sure he's planning on throwing me out of his life, I can't help but stare. His jaw is clenched, his shoulders are tense, but he still looks beautiful. Almost untouchable.

Finally, he stops in front of me. "Here's what's going to happen. We're going to go back to the house, and we're going to pretend like this conversation didn't happen. Understood?"

I nod, wiping away tears.

"Then we're going to let Tristan carry out his plan."

"What? Alexander, no!" I reach out for him, new tears forming in my eyes. When he snaps back from me, my heart completely shatters.

"Yes. We can't let him know that we're onto him, so we don't have a choice. Stop crying."

His words only make me sob harder. I sink down to the ground and pull my legs to my chest, burying my face into my knees. But I'm barely down five seconds before he's yanking me to my feet again.

"I don't want to lose you," I sob out, clutching his arms.

"Then get it together, Sophia. On the off chance that my house is bugged, or Tristan managed to get cameras in my house, we can't go back with you looking like this."

As I do my best to control my breathing, he pulls me against him. His arms are stiff around me, but I don't care. He's holding me. He's letting me touch him.

"Xan," I whisper, but he shushes me. My bottom lip starts quivering as he strokes my hair, but I take a few deep breaths to calm myself.

I can't let myself think that Tristan might win this. Can't focus on the hatred I saw in Xan's eyes mere minutes ago.

No. I have to trust him. He told me to take a leap of faith, and I did.

I just hope it's enough.

. . .

"Do you normally have this many events to go to?" I twirl my hair around my curling iron, glancing at Xander in the bathroom mirror.

He's just stepped out of the shower, and my stomach flutters as his gaze slides over me. "During summer and around the holidays. I know it's a lot."

"I'm sure I'll—" I cut myself off. Now that everything is out in the open, I *don't* know if I'll get used to attending events with Xander.

For all I know, this will be my last one by his side.

"You're going to burn your hair."

"Shit!" I release my hair from the curling iron and yank it away from my head. The curl falls onto my ear, burning hot.

Xander steps up behind me. Lightly, his hand touches my waist. "Are you all right?"

"Just distracted." I give him a smile in the mirror before moving on to the next strand of my hair.

He doesn't move. Instead, he fingers the light blue fabric of my dress. "You're not wearing this."

My heart practically stops. I know for a fact that this dress looks beautiful on me. "Excuse me?"

"You're wearing the yellow one." He leans into me until my hips are pinned to the counter. His erection presses against my back.

I let out a soft breath. Meeting his gaze in the mirror, I see a heat in them that's been missing since last night. "Xan . . ."

"You're wearing the yellow one, no questions asked. And later, I'm going to make sure the only thing you think of when you see that dress is me."

My cheeks are turning pink, and I know my eyes are wide with hope.

He wants me. *He wants me.* I'd say he's faking it in case Tristan is watching somehow, but if he was, Xan wouldn't be making me wear the dress.

And I can't deny the burning passion in his eyes. You can't fake that—you just can't.

Xander kisses my neck lightly before grabbing his towel and walking out.

Leaning against the counter, I do my best to catch my breath. I can still feel where he touched me. My skin burns with heat, the kind that only Xander has ever been able to pull out of me.

Maybe there still is hope.

I finish getting ready as quickly as I can before changing dresses. When I do my final check in the full-length mirror leaning against Xander's wall, I frown.

This shade of yellow really isn't my color. It's one of Rachel's old dresses, and she insisted I take it because the cut looks great on me. But the shade? Yuck.

With a sigh, I turn away from the mirror. At least my hair looks nice.

"Ready?" Xander says from the doorway.

"Sure." Grabbing my phone, I head over to him.

As we walk down to the garage, he keeps a hand on the small of my back. My heart skips a beat when he opens the car door for me and holds my little purse as I get inside.

Thankfully, the car ride to Everly's is silent. I don't know if I can handle trying to maintain a conversation while my head is racing as fast as my heart.

He still wants me.

But what if he's just performing?

Then why is he still acting possessive of me, if he doesn't care about me anymore?

I distract myself by scrolling through social media. Lissa has posted a few pictures of her cat, and Rachel and Victoria are happily sipping mimosas on a beach with their family.

My scroll stops when a picture of Dominic pops up. He's trailing behind a little girl riding a bike, holding onto the seat. The caption says, "Growing up too fast."

Narrowing my eyes, I tap on the profile of the woman who posted and tagged him in the photo—Jade Albright. The only mutual friend we have is Dominic, so she's not family with the Graysons. And I'd imagine that if they were dating, she'd be friends with Blaze.

I scroll through Jade's profile, but she has most of her posts private. So I head to Dominic's profile, even while thinking to myself that his personal life really isn't any of my business.

Once his profile loads, I frown. The picture of the little girl on the bike is gone. I refresh the page, since the photo was only posted a few minutes ago, but still nothing. And when I go back to Jade's profile, the photo has vanished there, too.

How odd.

The car comes to a stop, and I look up to see Everly's giant house sprawling before us. A giant banner hangs from a balcony overlooking the driveway. Big pink letters are sprawled across the white fabric, saying, "HAPPY BIRTHDAY, EVERLY!"

I cringe. It doesn't look classy, or nice, or any other words I'd use to describe the Hendricks mansion.

Xander is out of the car before I've even closed the apps on my phone. When he opens my door, he pauses, placing a hand on the roof of the car.

"I want you to know that no matter what happens, we'll be okay." He reaches out, brushing his fingers against my cheek. "Can you trust me?"

I nod, taking in the hint of worry on his features.

With that, he steps back, and we head inside. Soft music floats through the house, coming from the backyard. We make our way through the house slowly, and I take in the rooms as we go. Some of them are practically unchanged from when we were in high school. I have to stop myself from dragging Xan into the library for a secret makeout session, just like I used to.

But I spot Brooke outside on the patio, standing next to Blaze and Felix with stiff shoulders. Blaze has his arms around a woman with red hair, and I frown.

Just as I'm about to step outside, I feel a hand on my arm.

"Where do you think you're going?" Xander's breath is warm against my neck, but it sends shivers down my spine.

"I- uh, outside?"

"Not until I'm finished with you." He spins me around, placing a controlling hand on the back of my neck. "I promised to ruin you, and I'm a man of my word."

My eyes widen even as my stomach flutters. "Here?" I whisper, looking around. We're alone, but for how long?

With a smirk, Xander pulls me through a couple rooms before we end up in the laundry room. He closes the door quietly, but leaves it unlocked. When I reach for the doorknob, he grabs my wrist and whirls me around. My ass hits the washing machine as he holds my hands above my head.

"No matter what, you're mine. *Mine.* Do you understand that?"

"Yes. God, yes, Xander."

He kisses me, his free hand wrapping around my throat. It's unlike anything I've ever felt before. As his lips move against mine, it's like he's giving me air to breathe while simultaneously stealing it away. He's taking the best parts of me along with the worst, making sure every inch of me is his.

With a low groan, he pulls away. For a moment, he just stares at me. Then he hoists me onto the washer. He slides the straps of my dress off my shoulders and yanks it down, below my breasts. Without a moment's hesitation, he sucks a nipple into his mouth while his fingers tweak the other one, and I let out a gasp.

"Mine," he mumbles against my skin. His teeth graze against my nipple, causing me to shudder. "Only mine."

After what feels like an eternity of his tongue teasing my nipples, he reaches underneath my dress. A finger strokes up and down my soaked panties. I let out a tortured moan, squirming.

Finally, he pulls the thin strip of fabric to the side. He finds my clit with ease, giving it soft strokes as I fall back onto my elbows.

My first orgasm hits quickly. I've been on edge all day, and his teasing has me ready to explode. I'm barely able to contain my cry of pleasure as bolts of lightning shoot through me.

I glance at the door, but the thought of someone hearing us is lost on me when Xander leans down. His tongue circles my overly-sensitive clit, and my body jerks in response.

"Mine," he mutters again. His arms envelop me, pulling me closer to the edge of the washer. When his tongue flicks my clit again, it sends a shudder through me.

"Yours," I whisper. It sets off something in him, and his strokes turn violent. I bite my lip to keep my moans quiet, but when he thrusts three fingers into me, I almost come undone again.

He curls them just right, hitting a hyper-sensitive spot, while lightly sucking on my clit.

"Fuck, Xander," I groan. My head falls back, hitting the cabinet above the washer. He keeps going, curling his fingers and drawing circles on my clit with his tongue.

Just as I'm about to come, he pulls out. My legs are shaking, and my chest is heaving. When he undoes his shorts, yanking them down along with his boxers, I moan.

He steps forward, pausing to hold my face and kiss me.

"Is this real?" I whisper, placing my hands on his shoulders.

Pulling away slightly, his fiery gaze meets mine. "You tell me."

He lifts me off the washer, slowly lowering me onto his cock. We both groan, and I wrap my arms around his neck.

With his hands holding my ass, he moves me up and down. My hips grind to match his movements. He nibbles my neck before saying, "Does this feel real to you?"

"Yes," I cry as he bottoms out inside of me. I sway to one side as my eyes slide shut. My back hits a wall, and Xander shifts so it holds some of my weight.

His thrusts turn harder and faster, and one of his hands clamps over my mouth. "Will I ever have to remind you who you belong to again?"

I shake my head, moaning. I hear voices somewhere in the house, and my eyes go wide. But Xander just smirks, removing his hand from my mouth and snaking it in between our bodies.

"Can you stay quiet, little bird?" he murmurs as he flicks my clit with his thumb.

My fingernails dig into his shirt, and I bury my face into the crook of his neck. I'm close—*so close*.

Xander shifts me, angling my hips slightly differently. It changes everything, and a burst of pleasure causes me to scream into his shoulder. But he doesn't let up, even as my squirms make me impossibly hard to hold.

He shoves his thumb into my mouth, and I suck myself off of him. When he finally comes, it's with one last pump that shatters both of us.

He holds me as we both breathe heavily. After a few minutes, he sets me down gently, pulling my dress back up.

My body is still shaking as he sets me on the floor. As he peppers my neck with kisses, I hold onto his shirt for balance.

"Now we're ready to go outside," he says, nibbling the shell of my ear.

I adjust my dress as he pulls his shorts back up. "I need to clean myself up first. I'll meet you out there?"

He nods, giving me one more kiss before leaving. After taking a few deep breaths, I head down the hallway to one of the many bathrooms on the first floor. This one never got used as much, since it's a little out of the way.

Once I've locked myself inside, I work to clean myself up. When I glance in the mirror, I wince at my hair. It was perfect when we left, but now it's a mess.

I run my fingers through the soft curls, trying to smooth the frizz from my head rubbing against the laundry room wall.

When I finally look presentable enough, I make my way to the back of the house. But as I do, I find a large figure in my way.

He glares down at me with green eyes before pulling me into a sitting room.

"What the hell, Tristan?" I hiss, yanking my arm out of his hold.

"Ah, ah, ah, Sophia. Be careful how you treat me. Unless you want to say goodbye to your precious Xander, that is."

I freeze. I don't have to fake the fear in my voice as I say, "What do you want?"

"It's quite simple." He steps toward me, and I have to stop myself from backing away. "You know how Alexander never really got over you? Well, neither did I."

I can feel the blood draining out of my face as Tristan takes another step toward me, pulling one of my curls through his fingers.

"And considering you failed me last night, I'd say I'm owed some sort of compensation."

"What?" I whisper, clasping my hands together to hide the way they're shaking.

"Kiss me. Even more than that, kiss me like you mean it."

I laugh. "You can't be serious. I wouldn't kiss you if you were the last person on the planet."

He lets out an amused hum. "Even to save Alexander? I didn't expect you to give up so easily."

My stomach lurches. Of course, I should've expected this. Tristan is as manipulative as a person can get, and I swear he thrives off of making other people uncomfortable. I'd love nothing more than to wipe that disgusting smirk off his face right now.

Instead, I say, "Fine. But it has to be quick."

He wraps a hand around my waist. "It'll last as long as I want it to."

His lips meet mine, parting them. I place a hand on his shoulder, hiding my cringe as he runs his tongue across my bottom lip.

It doesn't matter. It's just a kiss. And it's not like you haven't kissed him before.

Tristan presses me closer to him, deepening the kiss. Forcing out a moan that's hopefully convincing, I follow his lead. Maybe if I act like I'm enjoying it, he'll end it sooner.

Finally, he pulls away, still holding me. "You taste better than I ever could've remembered."

I yank his arm away from me. "Now leave me alone."

As I storm past him, blinking back tears, he grabs my arm. "Not so fast, my love. Smile." He nods to a potted plant sitting on a table. Resting against it is a phone. "You're on camera."

Fuck. So this is his plan? Frame me for cheating, and then send Xander the evidence? Clever, I guess.

I widen my eyes, glancing between Tristan and the phone. I have to keep this believable.

"He'll never know what hit him," Tristan says, stalking toward the phone. Once it's in his hands, he smirks. "However, there's been a slight change to the plan."

"Tristan, please. Don't do this."

"I've already set everything into motion, my dear. Your Alexander has been getting in my way too much lately. So I've given him something to keep his time and thoughts occupied. Since, you know, you won't be anymore."

My heart sinks. *No.* "What are you talking about?"

Tristan steps forward, caressing my face. "If I were you, I'd go spend every precious second you have with your love. Because in a few hours, he'll be in jail. One down, three more to go."

Jail. Xander. No. No, no, *no*. "What the hell? I did what you asked. You told me you wouldn't do this."

"Did I?" Tristan laughs. "Well, it's quite simple. I lied."

"Soph?" Xander's voice floats through the house.

With a smirk, Tristan loops an arm around my waist. In my ear, he says, "You played your part well, Sophia. I wanted to draw this out longer, but your boyfriend had to fuck things up."

Xander steps into the room and freezes. His eyes rest on Tristan's hand on my waist, holding me close. And while his face is unreadable, it does nothing to soothe my nerves.

"Oops," Tristan says, releasing me. "Looks like your real boyfriend is here. I'll see you later, love." He brushes past Xander with a smirk.

For a moment, Xander and I just stare at each other. Then he steps forward, brushing his fingers down my arm. "Are you okay?"

"You need to leave." The words come out of my mouth before I've even fully processed them.

Xander frowns. "What?"

"Tristan, he has something on you. He said he's getting you arrested. Today. Can you leave the country or something? Xander, what does he have on you? What's going on?"

Grabbing his arms, I stare up into his eyes. Soft, brown, comforting—that's what I was hoping to find. Instead, they're hard and cold. Calculating.

Xander may have only come back into my life a couple weeks ago, but I'll be damned if I lose him. And as I watch him, it's like I'm transported back to senior year. To the last time he treated me with warmth before all he gave me was that cold, hard stare.

"Xander," I whisper.

He runs a hand through my hair. "I meant what I said earlier. No matter what happens, we'll be okay. Just trust me. Okay?"

I gulp, and my fingers tighten around his arms. But I nod, watching him, hoping for a spark of warmth or love or compassion.

All he gives me is a light kiss on the forehead. It's all we have time for, before his phone pings. When he pulls it out, I let out a short breath. It's a message from Tristan—a video.

With a sigh, Xander leans his forehead against mine. "Is this what I think it is?"

"He tricked me," I whisper.

"I know, sweetheart. I know. Now go outside, and stand with Brooke and the guys. And get ready to perform. Okay?"

When he kisses me, it's with such longing that I have no doubt Xander and I are on the same page. We belong together, like the moon belongs to the sun. And nothing will stop us from chasing after each other.

He finally releases me with a low groan. I have no desire to leave him, but the gentle nudge he gives me sends me outside.

Brooke is standing uncomfortably next to Blaze. Her eyes dart anywhere except him and the redhead he's holding in his arms. When she sees me, relief floods her expression.

"Hey." I wrap her up in my arms, frowning at the tension in her body as she hugs me back. "How are you doing?"

She shrugs. "Mostly better. Just a dull headache. Oh, and trying to get to sleep is a nightmare. I don't even trust my own house anymore."

"I thought Blaze is staying with you." I give him a glance, and he grins at me. Turning back to Brooke, I say quietly, "And I could've sworn he had a thing for you."

"He's engaged," she says, turning back to face the rest of the guys.

Raising an eyebrow, I take in the beauty standing on the other side of Blaze. She's tall, and much fuller than Brooke. Her hair flows past her shoulders in perfect waves, kissing her bare back.

I can't deny that she's sexy as hell. But she doesn't strike me as Blaze's type. He's always gone for the softer girls—the ones who are more into books and art and sweaters. Not the ones who're into fashion and makeup and social status.

Maybe she's into both, I tell myself. *A woman can be however many things she fucking wants to be.*

Still, I hate how uncomfortable Brooke is. I'm about to ask her if she wants to find some place to hide, but Xander storming down the steps catches my eye.

"What the fuck is this?" he yells, fury in his eyes. It takes him mere seconds to get to me and yank me away from the group. Shoving his phone in my face, he grips my arm and forces me to watch.

It's the video of Tristan and I kissing, edited so the part where he forced me has been cut out.

Looking up at Xander in horror, I step back. So *this* is what he meant when he told me to get ready to perform. In front of all these people—including Tristan.

"Xan, please don't do this. I can explain."

"You can *explain?* There's no way to explain this, Soph. You cheated on me. Have you been the entire time? We're over. Done."

I open my mouth, but no words come out. Instead I let my eyes blur over, tears flooding from the embarrassment. *Everyone* is watching.

Turning to Dominic, Xander mutters, "I'll bring her things over later."

"Tristan?" Brooke hisses next to me. Her eyes are burning with a mixture of hatred and disbelief.

"It's not what it looks like, I promise."

Everly appears next to Xander, slipping her arm through his. The smile on her face makes me sick. "Are you all right, Alex?"

He shakes her off, glaring at me. "I'll be fine once she's out of my sight."

I'm so caught up in the terrifyingly-convincing ice in Xander's eyes that I almost don't see them. But their black uniforms catch my attention as they move in on us.

Or, more accurately, Xander.

"Alexander Hendricks?" one of the police officer says, standing behind him. "You're under arrest for the murder of Francis Hendricks."

CHAPTER 14

Alexander

There are certain times in my life that are a blur.

Parts of my childhood. Most of my senior year. Summers home during my college years. And now, the past few days.

Somehow, I got out on bail. Probably because the evidence against me is pitiful and I have a rock-solid alibi. Oh, and the best lawyer in the entire city.

Tristan released a photo of me with my father on his boat to the police. It wasn't even on the day he died, although there was a timestamp that said it was.

I should be focused on proving my innocence. On getting this goddamned tracker off my ankle. But when my lawyers aren't bugging me, or Brooke isn't fussing over me, my thoughts only go to one place.

Sophia.

Her blue eyes were swimming with tears the last time I saw her. Sure, our fight had been staged, but I still accused her of cheating on me in front of everyone at my mom's party. But there hadn't been another way. I had to make sure Tristan saw.

My plan had been to soothe her personally, as soon as I could after the party. But of course Tristan just had to sic the police on me.

It's an interesting strategy, I'll give him that. It's definitely kept me distracted and off his case. But I'm done. Tristan thinks he won, and he can continue to think that for now. It just gives me an edge.

"Done." Felix's voice cuts through my thoughts. He's standing a few feet away from me, hands shoved into his pockets.

I get up from my spot on the couch. God knows how long I've been sitting here. "Did you find anything?"

He nods. "He had bugs in most rooms. I did a pretty thorough sweep, but I can have one of the guys go through everything again if it'd make you feel better."

Shaking my head, I say, "I'm sure you got it all. You're good at what you do. So we're able to talk freely now?"

He nods, his lips pressed together into a thin line.

"I want to see Sophia. And we need to get our shit together. If Tristan is going to keep pulling stunts like this, we're in trouble."

Felix nods grimly. "At least we had the foresight to make sure you had an alibi the day of your father's death."

With a sigh, I pick up my phone to text Dom. "I don't care about that. This is just a distraction. We need to take Tristan and David down, and we need to do it quickly."

Felix watches me closely. "You're not planning on doing anything stupid, are you?"

I pause, meeting his gaze. Felix is sharp—of course he hasn't forgotten that I suggested killing them a few days ago. But Dominic is right. We need to take down their whole operation, otherwise their trafficking gig will just continue without them. "I'm not going to kill them. Not yet."

Nodding, Felix plucks my phone out of my hands. "Dominic is already on the way with Sophia. Same with Blaze and Brooke. Just sit tight."

I run a hand through my hair. "I can't. I need to see her. And I need to get her out of this. Have we made any progress?"

"Yes, actually. We have someone on the inside at David's house. He has a fairly predictable schedule, so she's planning on getting me inside so we can go through his office."

"Who the hell do you have?"

"His maid." Felix begins pacing in front of the TV. "We can trust her. For now, at least."

I narrow my eyes, watching him. His shoulders are a bit tense, and his hands are still deep in his pockets. "How do we know that?"

For a moment, Felix stops. Then he turns to face me. "She owes me a favor."

"That's one hell of a coincidence."

He shakes his head. "She has some motive of her own. I'm not sure what, but she's willing to help us."

"That doesn't mean she's on our side, though. She's on her own." Dominic's voice causes both of us to turn. He's standing next to Sophia, whose eyes are trained on me. "But we both have a common enemy. That's what matters."

"Soph." I rush to her, pulling her into my arms. She only relaxes a little before pulling away to kiss me on the cheek.

All of a sudden, the rest of the world fades. The only thing I care about is getting Sophia upstairs and reminding her that she's *mine*—forever.

I tangle my fingers through her blonde strands and keep her tucked under my arm. She's been staying with Dominic ever since my mother's birthday party, and I've hated every second apart from her.

"Don't worry about Tristan and David. We'll handle them. You two just stay safe," Felix says, his eyes on me.

"What about this murder charge?" Sophia asks, her voice small. She glances between the three of us, her eyes wide.

An uncomfortable silence fills the room. We've managed to keep this truth from Sophia for long enough. Too long, if you ask Dominic. But I'm just not ready to break it to her yet.

"I'm working on it." Felix's voice is gentle. "The photo wasn't taken the day of Francis's accident. I know because I took it, a few weeks beforehand. We'd all been together at a family gathering on the beach."

"So you—you can prove that the timestamp was edited?" The hope in Sophia's voice almost breaks me. She's been through so much the past couple weeks. Too much.

Once again, my argument with Dominic weeks earlier comes back to haunt me. I should've waited to bring Sophia back into this. If I lose her—if anything happens to her—I'll never forgive myself. *Never.*

"I can," Felix says with a grin. "Put a computer under my hands, and I can make her do anything I please."

Dominic snorts. "Notice how he said *her*. He's so touch-starved that he's turning to technology for love."

With a playful show of his middle finger, Felix says, "Here's the thing. Women can play you—computers can't. Maybe you should give them a try."

That shuts Dominic up. His face darkens, and he clenches his jaw. Felix may be close with Dominic, but that was still a low blow.

Not too long ago, Dom had walked in on his girlfriend fucking another man. He'd been head over heels. About to propose, even. Just to find out that the supposed love of his life was only using him to get to a colleague. A few months have passed, but it's pretty obvious that Dominic isn't over it yet.

"Shit, man. I'm sorry. It was too soon."

Dominic shakes his head, waving off Felix's apology. "Forget about it. Have you set a date with Willow? We need more intel."

"This weekend. Supposedly David is leaving town for a few days. It gives me the best chance to hack into his security system and snoop around without getting caught."

Dominic frowns. It's a long time to wait, considering David attacked Brooke, and Tristan is trying to get me in prison. Who knows what else they have up their sleeves? But Felix getting caught—that's a risk none of us are willing to take.

"Fill me in on the details later," I say, slipping my hand into Sophia's. I tug, and she follows me out of the room with only a moment of hesitation.

Once we're in my bedroom, I lock the door. "Felix swept the house and found a couple bugs. We can speak freely now. And you can move back in."

She looks at me silently, still tense. Understandably. Stepping toward me, her fingers twist into my hoodie. "Are you okay? Can Felix really fix this?"

I place my hands on her shoulders, gazing down at her. Worry has her brows furrowed, her lips pressed together tightly. I can't have that. "I told you, little bird. We'll be okay. Just trust me."

She lets out a small sigh, slipping her arms around my waist. Electricity shoots through me as she rests her forehead against my chest. One touch from this woman, no matter how small, sends me reeling.

Even though I know Tristan forced her into that kiss, I still hated watching it. Yet I did—I watched it over and over again, each time my fury rising a little bit more.

That man is disgusting, and he had his hands all over Sophia. His lips had touched hers, in what had been way too long of a kiss. The bastard had enjoyed it. Enjoyed *her*.

He's going to pay. But right now, I have Sophia pressed against me. Clinging to me. And what I need—what we both need—is *us*.

So I lift her chin with two fingers and press my lips against hers. The involuntary moan that sounds in her throat sends another jolt of electricity through me. I deepen our kiss, capturing all of her attention, all of her desires.

She's *mine*, and I need to prove it. To her. To myself.

"Xander," she whispers, so softly it makes me lose every ounce of self control.

One moment, my lips are moving against hers, tasting as much of her as I can. The next, she's on the bed, under me, while I tear off her clothes.

She says my name again, breathlessly, and I silence her with my mouth on hers. She tastes like chocolate, like sweetness.

"Never kiss another man again," I say darkly, my hand fisting her hair.

"I won't," she pants. "I promise."

"And never lie to me again. I won't let it go so easily next time, little bird."

I feel her shiver underneath me. "I didn't want to," she whispers.

When I look down, there are tears in her eyes. One falls onto her cheek, and I lean down and lick it away.

The truth is, I know she couldn't help it. She was scared and cornered. Just thinking about it makes me want to punch a wall.

Instead, I murmur, "I know," and kiss her.

When she moves to pull off my shirt, I catch her wrists in mine. "No, let me. I want you—all of you, Xan." She tries to free her hands, but I keep them firmly in my grip as she squirms under me.

"Soon," I say, my voice low. Then I get my arms under her and throw her so her head hits the pillows. Before she has a chance to scramble up, I'm on her again, grabbing the soft ropes sitting on my nightstand.

Her eyes widen, and she gives one last attempt at getting my hoodie off before I pin her arms above her head. Before I tie her up, I kiss her again, stealing her breath along with her willpower. She stills beneath me. Her back arches, and the moan that escapes her mouth almost kills me.

This woman. *My* woman. I need to see her writhing underneath my touch, hear her screaming my name. I need to watch her as pleasure takes her under, sends her soaring.

I make quick work of the rope, tying her wrists to the headboard. And while I desperately need to touch her, to lick every inch of her beautiful skin, I stop myself. Settling back, I take her in.

Her hair spills over the dark pillows, framing her face. She's panting, her pale breasts falling as her chest heaves. And her neck—god, her neck, open and vulnerable and waiting for me to wrap my fingers around it.

I almost do, but I let my eyes trail over her stomach, her legs, her soaked core. Perfect. She's perfect.

When I kiss her, it's with a fierceness that surprises even me. Sophia has been consuming every spare thought I've had over the past few days, and now she's here, practically begging for my touch.

She gasps when I pull away, only for her to moan as I lean down and lick one of her nipples. Her hips grind against mine as I circle my finger around her other nipple, not quite touching, just teasing.

After switching, I drag my mouth down her stomach. She whimpers and begs, her legs parting on their own. I give her clit a single lick before straightening.

"Xander, what—oh, god, please don't stop. Xan, please."

"In time, little bird." I pull off my sweatpants and underwear quickly, not once taking my eyes off the beauty tied up beneath me. "In time."

My dick is already rock-hard, and she licks her lips at the sight of it. But before she can have it, I wrap my fingers around her throat. Her eyes flutter closed as I apply just the lightest bit of pressure. When I kiss her, her moan vibrates under my hand.

"Please, Xander," she whispers against my lips.

With a smile, I crawl farther over her, until the tip of my cock is touching her lips. I don't even have to tell her what to do. Her tongue flicks out, tasting my skin and the precum dripping from me. When she takes me into her mouth, I groan. It's hot, and wet, and I've never wanted to fuck her face more than I do right now.

But I stay perfectly still, watching her head bob up and down as she takes more of me in. Her lips look perfect wrapped around my cock. Perfect and fuckable.

"Soph," I moan, my gaze locking onto hers. Her head slows, and she looks up at me with wide eyes. That's it. I can't take it anymore.

With one hand on the headboard and the other with a fistful of hair at the back of her head, I take over. I start slowly, not wanting to hurt her. But the farther I push myself into her mouth, the more of her I need.

She adjusts her head slightly. At first I think she wants me to pull out, but when she presses forward, I realize it's the exact opposite of that.

Fuck me.

I pick up my pace, thrusting into her until I reach the back of her throat. I watch her face as tears form in her eyes, but she continues watching me with a greedy satisfaction.

God, if she keeps looking at me like that, I'm going to come way too fast.

Pleasure builds up inside of me, and I slow down for a few thrusts. Fuck—*fuck*. I can see it in Sophia's eyes just how much she loves this. Just how much she wants this.

"I'm going to come in your mouth, little bird," I say, picking up my pace again. "And don't you dare swallow."

She moans, her eyes finally closing. I finish with a grunt, filling her mouth until my cum is dripping from her lips. When I pull out, I hold her jaw open, taking her in. There's no denying that she's mine now.

I grab my phone and snap a picture. For the next time I feel the need to remind her that I've claimed her—for good.

Finally, I let her swallow, wiping her face clean of me with a tissue. "Do you need some water, little bird?"

She nods, still panting. I snatch my empty water glass from my nightstand and fill it up in the bathroom sink. After helping her take a few sips, I plant a kiss on her swollen lips.

Then, with a nibble on her ear, I whisper, "I'm going to make you come so many times, you won't even remember your own name."

"Wait," she blurts, her eyes widening. "I need to tell you something."

I stare at her, every moment of silence like a band tightening around my chest. "What?" I finally grunt out.

She takes a deep breath, trying to squirm into a sitting position, but I keep her pinned down.

"Spit it out," I snap. My heart is beating rapidly, and she's going to send me into a full-on panic attack if she doesn't start talking.

"Xan, I've—I've wanted to say it for a while now, but I wanted to wait until you knew I really meant it. I didn't want you to think that he was making me say it." Her wide eyes meet mine as she takes another breath. "Xan, I love you. I love you so much my heart can barely take it sometimes."

Fuck. The tension in my chest dissipates, and I lean down to brush my lips against hers. "I know, little bird. I've known for a while now."

"I'm sorry for scaring you," she whispers, her eyes still wide. "And for lying to you. I promise I won't do it again."

I chuckle. "Don't worry, I'll make you pay."

She whimpers, squirming under me. I take her breasts into my hands, rubbing my thumbs over her pebbled nipples. She gasps, probably so turned on and needy that she feels like she'll burst.

Good. I want this to feel as amazing as possible.

I work her nipples until she's practically sobbing, begging for more. Her wrists are still tied, but that doesn't stop the rest of her from moving. When I suck one of her nipples into my mouth, her back arches. She pulls at her restraints, but it's useless.

Eventually, I lay next to her, spreading her legs. She gasps as my finger brushes against her clit. She's soaked—so, so soaked. *For me.*

Her head lolls back into the pillows as I lick the closest nipple to me. Even if she wasn't tied up right now, I don't think she'd be able to do a thing. From a single finger and my tongue, she's lost all control of her own body.

It's mine now, to do whatever I want to it.

And what I want is to push her over the edge.

I soak in her body, laying before me like a feast. Her chest heaves as I graze her nipple with my teeth. Her whole body jerks as I run my finger over her clit, in up and down and circular motions.

She's lost in a feeling of pure bliss, her eyes closed, her legs spread wide for me. She lets out a series of small moans, each one more and more tense.

"That's it, little bird," I whisper in her ear. "You're going to come for me, again and again and again."

She cries out, her body jerking and flailing as her first orgasm takes over. I barely let up, too entrenched in the look on her face to stop. When she's finished, I kiss her gently.

Pulling at the ropes, she tries to sit up. But I shove her back down, saying, "I'm not done with you yet."

And I'm not. Truth is, I never will be.

I'll do whatever it takes to prove it.

Chapter 15

Sophia

When I wake up, I'm in bed alone. The sky has darkened, but the lamp on the bedside table glows softly.

With a smile, I ease myself into a sitting position. I'm sore, but I've never felt this satisfied before.

After a while, I lost track of everything—the time, the fact that the Graysons were downstairs, how many times I came—*everything*.

I find my clothes and slip them on. It's chilly without the covers from the bed covering me, so I grab one of Xander's hoodies. I have a feeling he won't mind.

Downstairs, everyone is settled in the living room. Well, everyone except Brooke. She's standing by the mantle, arms wrapped around her waist, staring out the window.

"Ah, you're awake." Dominic grins at me, a sparkle in his eyes.

Blushing, I lower myself onto the couch next to Xander, just to get pulled onto his lap. He plants a kiss on my hairline.

Dominic leans back in his chair. "We were just finishing up our plans. Felix is at the office working to prove that the photo of Alex is fake. We have a few leads to take down Tristan and David. Mainly, David's maid and a few guys who are going to tail them."

I narrow my eyes. "You don't think they know how to watch their backs?"

"Oh, on the contrary, they do. We've tried simply following them before, but it hasn't worked. So we're setting up a more . . . complex system. No one car will be on their tail long enough for them to get suspicious."

Clever. I've never thought of using multiple cars to follow someone before—probably because I've never needed to.

"We'll take them down soon enough, sweetheart. Until then, I want you here with me. You'll be safe."

"What if Tristan finds out?" I shiver. After he gave up the leverage he had over me, I thought my fear of him would fade. But it hasn't. Not one bit.

"Let him." Blaze leans forward, placing his elbows on his knees and clasping his hands. "He has nothing over you two anymore. All we need to worry about is clearing Alex's name and keeping you two safe. Both should be a piece of cake for us."

Sighing, I lean into Xander. His arms come around me and hold me close. A piece of cake. A piece of cake? "They've already broken into two of our houses. How can this be easy?"

Xander chuckles. "Your house isn't exactly a fortress."

"And I forgot to set my alarm the night David broke into my house." Brooke turns to face us. It's the first time she's spoken since I walked in.

"Which won't happen again," Blaze says, shooting her a dark look. She rolls her eyes and turns away.

"We'll make sure you're safe, Soph," Dominic says. "And Blaze isn't leaving Brooke's side. Just trust us, okay? Protecting people is what we do for a living."

I nod, staring at the floor. Trust. After all they've hidden from me for the past few weeks? Dominic caught me up to speed on Tristan and David's operation, but it still feels like I don't have the whole story.

Blaze stands. "Actually, I was thinking we should head home. That okay with you, Brooke?"

She turns to look at me and Xander. "You're sure this is all going to get cleared up? I don't want this to be the last time I see Alex not behind bars."

"I'll be fine." Xander's voice is deep and calm, without a hint of worry. "It's a bullshit accusation anyway."

Blaze and Dominic share a look with each other. Xander's grip around my waist tightens and doesn't relax until we're standing to walk everyone out.

At the door, Dominic turns to Xander. "Sophia should come home with me. She's safer there until we can upgrade your security. And all of her stuff is there."

I'm about to protest, but he places a finger over my lips. "One night."

With a tight hug, I leave with Dominic. It only takes a few minutes to get to his house. The whole time, I sit in silence, question after question flitting through my mind.

Yet whenever I open my mouth to ask one, I stop myself. Dominic has already told me everything he thinks I need to know. He's always been so cool-headed. Measured. No amount of begging or pestering is going to get him to open up.

My only option is to trust them.

Once we're inside, Dominic lets out a long breath. "I'm going to make myself some tea and read for a bit. Do you want any?"

"Sure," I say, settling onto one of the stools at his kitchen counter.

I watch as he fills the tea kettle and lights the stove. It's been so long since I've spent time with Dominic. The last week or so has been nice, but weird—just like now. The silence between us isn't heavy, but it's not relaxed, either. And if he's worried about Xander, he's not showing it. Instead, he moves calmly, fluidly, as he gets two mugs and teabags.

It looks like he's about to say something when the doorbell rings, followed by pounding on the door. A small, high-pitched voice cries out. "Mister Dominic! Mister Dominic, please help!"

Tossing the mugs onto the counter, Dominic rushes to the door and yanks it open. A little girl, no older than six, stands on the porch in a purple nightgown.

"Rosie, what's wrong?" Dominic kneels down, taking her hands in his.

She bursts into tears. "It-it's Auntie. She's breathing funny, and she—" Rosie starts sobbing, her face scrunching up.

The color drains from Dominic's face. Scooping Rosie into his arms, he takes off, heading for the house across the street. I follow, grateful we didn't even have time to take off our shoes yet.

"Where is she?" Dominic asks as he crosses the threshold into the house.

Rosie points. "Please don't let her die."

"Jade," Dominic shouts, running up the stairs and down a hallway. He sets Rosie down and rushes into a room.

Jade. That's the woman who posted that picture of Dominic online, just for it to disappear.

I hear a startled cry, and then Dominic's soothing voice. Rosie stands in the doorway, still sobbing. When I reach her, I find Dominic checking over a woman who's sitting on the floor next to a bed.

She's looking at Dominic with a hollow, red-eyed stare that I'd recognize anywhere. Her breaths are shallow and quick.

"Jade, what's wrong? What's going on?" Dominic strokes her brown hair back from her face.

"She's having a panic attack," I say, kneeling next to Rosie. I squeeze the little girl's shoulder, whispering, "She's gonna be okay. I promise."

"What do you need?" Dominic's voice is calm. "Do you want me to stay with you?"

Tears are streaming down Jade's face, but she manages to nod. Dominic sits next to her, putting an arm around her, stroking her cheek.

"Auntie," Rosie whimpers. She leans into me, but she doesn't take her eyes off of Jade's shaking form.

"She's gonna be okay, Rosie," Dominic says, giving her a quick glance. Then his attention is back to Jade. "You can get through this. I know you can."

Rosie turns and runs from the room, still sobbing. I follow, worried that hearing her crying will just make Jade feel worse. She disappears into a room with pink walls, a nightlight illuminating her face. As she plops onto the floor, she grabs a stuffed bunny and hugs it to her chest.

After a few sobs, she throws the bunny onto the floor. "This is all daddy's fault. He called her, and then she started crying and breathing funny."

I frown. "Your dad?"

"He makes her cry every day."

Biting my lip, I squeeze her hand. "I know it's hard. But just know that Jade is gonna be okay."

Rosie looks up at me with the biggest, most innocent brown eyes I've ever seen. "I want to move away."

"To get away from your dad?"

She nods. "I hate him."

I raise my eyebrows. That's a strong word for a little kid. But I don't deny it's what she's feeling.

I stay with Rosie until she's done crying. She curls up in my lap, sniffling, until her breaths even. When I look down, her eyes are closed, and her features have relaxed.

Eventually, Dominic pops his head through the doorway. His features are solemn, but they soften at the sight of Rosie sleeping in my arms. "I have to go."

He lifts Rosie out of my arms and settles her on her bed. "I need you to lock yourself up in the house and sit tight for a while."

Fear spikes through my chest. "What's wrong?"

"It doesn't matter. Let's just go."

I follow him out of the house, watching his tense shoulders. "It's Xan, isn't it?"

"Soph-"

"I'm coming with you," I blurt, and before he can protest, I jump into his car. "Fighting with me will just slow you down."

For a moment, he glares at me like he wants to strangle me. But then he just shakes his head, sighs, and gets in. "I'm going to regret this."

CHAPTER 16

Alexander

I sit in the living room for god knows how long, just staring at my reflection in the dark windows. It may be late, but sleep won't be happening soon. Not when Sophia isn't next to me.

At some point, I find myself in swim trunks, heading outside and diving into the pool. For as long as I can remember, swimming has always helped me to clear my head.

Lap after lap, I let the water calm me.

Thoughts of Sophia clog my mind. Our first-ever kiss. The time I was wrenched out of my car and thought I'd never see her again. When I broke up with her and it almost killed me. In the club, when I pulled her onto my lap and she relaxed into me. Or earlier today, when she tried to hold back her screams, but she couldn't.

No matter how much I've tried, I can't get my heart to feel the way it feels for Sophia for any other woman. And believe me, I've tried.

But I'm hers, wholly. I always have been. And I always will be.

When I get out of the pool, my body is finally feeling tired. Unfortunately, my mind is as fucked up as ever.

As I towel off, I take deep, measured breaths. I force my thoughts off into a different direction—my childhood, playing with Brooke and the Grayson brothers.

Looking back, it seemed like every day that we would escape to the Grayson house. It was either that or try to find a place in the house where we couldn't hear our parents fighting.

I sigh. Of course my happiest childhood memories are tainted by my father. What isn't? He was always in the background, being his asshole self. And no matter how much I tried to protect Brooke from him, he still got to her.

Still told her she wasn't pretty enough, wasn't thin enough, would never *be* enough. The way he treated her still disgusts me, even though he'll never be able to hurt her again.

My fists clench around my towel. *Fuck.* How am I going to tell Sophia the truth? What if she never sees me the same again?

"I never thought of you as much of a deep thinker, Hendricks."

I spin around to see Tristan standing on the other side of the pool.

How the hell did he get this close to the house without tripping off any of the motion sensors? I glance at my phone on the table. I should've gotten a notification.

That's right—I put it on silent earlier so nothing would disturb me and Sophia.

Just stay calm. The Graysons will get notifications of an intruder.

"Probably because you're not one yourself." Throwing my towel onto the ground, I cross my arms. *No weapon. No protection. Great.* "What the hell are you doing here?"

"Oh, just giving you a little warning, since you won't be able to do anything about it anyway." Tristan circles the pool, coming closer.

I stay silent, watching his every movement.

"You've always thought you're better than I am. During school, in business, everywhere. Hell, you even managed to steal Sophia from me."

That's because you're an asshole.

"I loved her, more than you'll ever know."

I bark out a laugh. "*Loved* her? If I'm remembering correctly—and I know I am—she was terrified of you."

"Because you poisoned her against me," Tristan snaps, coming to stand in front of me. His hands are shoved in his pockets. "It's about time I do the same to you. Although—" He looks around with a smirk. "I don't see her here. Couldn't get over the fact that she prefers me now, huh?"

"Leave Sophia out of this," I say, my voice low and even.

"Of course you don't think she deserves the truth. She was in love with a *murderer*."

"Leave. her. out. of. this."

With a cruel smile twisting his face, Tristan takes another step forward. "I don't have to involve her, Alexander. You already did. I know you murdered your father. And I'll do whatever it takes to prove it. After that? Think how Sophia will feel about herself. She fell in love with a cold-blooded killer. She'll never trust her judgment again."

My blood runs cold. The Graysons and I covered up Francis's murder perfectly—right down to me having a solid alibi. But the idea that we missed something has always lingered in the back of my head.

If I go to prison, fine. But Sophia getting hurt in the process? That I will never, *ever* be okay with.

My fist meets Tristan's jaw before I even realize what I'm doing. He stumbles back, bringing a hand to his face.

"Beat me all you want," he says, straightening. "I'll find what I need to prove that you're responsible for Francis's death."

He swings at me, but I dodge easily—just for him to kick me right in the knee.

I hit the ground, ignoring the way the pavement scrapes at my skin. All of my focus is on the knife Tristan just pulled from his jacket.

"I may need you alive, but that doesn't mean I can't hurt you."

That's when I see her. Her eyes are wide, her blonde hair shining in the moonlight. And the fear on her face? I don't think I'll ever be able to wash that from my memory.

Dominic is moving in, a gun in his hands.

Some men would hate the idea of being rescued. Some men would get up from their knees and fight, knife be damned.

But me? Maybe I'm more in control of my ego. Smarter. Or maybe I'm a coward. But I stay right where I am. And when Tristan lunges for me, Dominic doesn't hesitate to shoot.

The knife clatters to the ground. Tristan clutches his chest, gasping as blood stains his shirt. Without hesitation, I scramble to my feet and yank him up.

When my fist hits the spot on his shirt stained with blood, he screams. I do it again, for Sophia, and then shove him backwards.

He falls into the water with no more than a pathetic grunt.

Blaze comes crashing through the patio door, weapon in hand. "What the hell happened?" He stops next to me, staring at the man thrashing in the pool below us. "Fuck."

Dominic joins us, and we watch as Tristan's body stills.

And it hits me.

Sophia.

Turning, I find her frozen solid, her feet planted where she was when I first saw her. When my eyes meet hers, she stumbles backward.

"Sophia—"

She turns and runs before I can get another word out. I chase after her, calling out her name, cursing myself as she disappears around a corner.

I catch up to her with ease, grabbing her arm and wrenching her toward me. She does her best to squirm away, beating at my chest.

"You killed him," she shouts, tears falling from her eyes.

Grabbing both of her arms, I pin them at her sides. "He deserved to die."

She lets out a sharp laugh. Bitter. Afraid. "And you're the one who gets to decide that? Why did you push him into the pool?" As she says the words, she starts to struggle again, but I shove her against the house.

"Why didn't you jump in to save him?" My voice is calm, the meaning behind my words ruthless. *You wanted him dead, too.*

Sophia stills, letting out a small breath. She glares up at me, and even though her tears are still flowing and her chest is heaving from panic, I can't stop thinking about her lips. Perfect, pink, small. So sweet.

"Fuck you," she whispers.

"You know I'm not a good person, little bird. You fell for me anyway."

She winces, and I regret my words immediately.

She'll never trust her judgment again.

Her voice breaks as she says, "I wish I never had."

CHAPTER 17

Sophia

I feel sick as Dominic drives me back to his house.

Watching Dominic shoot Tristan? It was terrible, yes, but Dom did what he had to do to save Xan. But watching Tristan drown? Watching him *die?*

I shiver. I don't know how anyone could look at another human being and decide to end their life.

As if he can read my mind, Dominic clears his throat. "Please just remember that Tristan was a man who literally kidnapped children and sold them into sex slavery."

I nod. Maybe Xander is right—Tristan deserved to die. Hell, he probably deserved worse. But who are we to decide that?

"As for Francis . . ." Dominic grimaces.

We'd made it to Xander's backyard just in time to hear Tristan talking about Francis's death. More specifically, how Xander had killed him.

"I thought he crashed his boat and fell off while he was drunk," I say, my voice small. But even as the words leave my mouth, it all clicks into place.

No witnesses. Easy enough to fake if you know what you're doing.

"Francis was a terrible man, Soph. He hurt Everly. And you saw what he did to Brooke when we were kids."

I sink down into my seat. "He also destroyed my father."

As I stare at the passing houses, a thought slips into my head, unwarranted and unwanted. *What if Xander killed him for me?*

The timing adds up. Xander made it clear that Francis was the reason we had to break up. And not even six months after his death, there was Xander, invading my life and taking up all of my spare thoughts.

However much I hate the thought of Xander murdering people, there's a part of me that craves the safety of loving a man who'll go to the ends of the earth to keep me safe.

But it's not enough. Xander is a cold-blooded killer. And I want *nothing* to do with a man like that.

Once we're back at Dominic's house, I disappear into my room and lock the door. The Graysons convinced Xander to spend the night here, just in case David comes around, and I have no desire to see him.

Not now, and not ever again.

Right now, I only care about one thing: getting the hell out of here.

As I throw all my things into my bag, I fight the tears that are threatening to spill over. I can't cry right now. Not until I'm back home, in my own bed, far away from the monster who managed to con his way back into my heart.

Once the house is quiet, I sneak into the hallway. Dominic gave me the code for the security system in case I ever wanted to go outside, so now I just have to make it to the keypad unseen.

And based on the darkness enveloping me, everyone must be asleep.

Still, I tiptoe through the house, peering into every room before entering. As I make it to the living room, my phone vibrates with a notification. My ride must be here.

I step into the room and freeze. Alexander sits on the couch, his elbows on his knees, his lips pressed to his interlaced fingers. He's so deep in thought he doesn't even notice as I pass behind him.

When I reach the keypad, I bite my lip. He'll *definitely* hear it beep, and there's no way I'll be able to open and close the door without alerting him.

But it's the only way I can get out of here, and I *need* to leave.

I just hope he lets me.

As soon as I hit the last button on the keypad, I rush to the door, cringing at the loud *beep*. I hear a rustle, and then footsteps, but I focus on getting the door open.

"What the hell are you doing?"

Even as I'm turning, I hate myself for looking back. Alexander is standing there, still fully dressed, with a gun in his hands. My eyes widen at the sight, and he quickly shoves it into the waistband of his jeans.

"Close the door, Sophia. You're not going anywhere."

"You can't stop me. And please don't try."

It may be dark, but I can still see the pain in his eyes. But when I step through the doorway, he doesn't move to stop me. And when I close it behind me, I breathe a sigh of relief when I hear the lock sliding back into place.

I run to the car waiting at the edge of the yard, smiling at the driver as I climb in. And it's only when we're out of Dominic's neighborhood that I finally let the tears start to fall.

For the heartbreak five years ago, and the heartbreak today. For myself, and my shattered heart. And for my innocence, and my goodness, that apparently aren't as strong as I thought they were.

As much as I hate him, Tristan was right. I fell in love with a monster, and I don't know if I'll ever trust myself again.

CHAPTER 18

Sophia

Two weeks later

"That's six-fifty, please." I smile at the man on the other side of the counter as he fishes out his card and swipes. "It'll be just a minute."

I grab his coffee and pumpkin muffin, almost dropping them both when I see the tall, dark-haired man behind him. *Alexander.*

"You okay, ma'am?" The man in front of me frowns. He's young, his blond hair falling into his blue, blue eyes that remind me of Blaze.

Blaze, and everyone else—including the unstoppable force currently staring me down. With a shudder, I grip the edge of the counter.

"Ma'am?" the man asks again, leaning forward. "Do you need to sit down? You look sick. I can help you to a chair if you'd like."

"I'll take it from here." Alexander's voice cuts through the air. His sharp gaze lands on the blond man in front of me, harsh and intimidating.

To his credit, the man hesitates before giving me a small nod and leaving. If I didn't know who Alexander was, I wouldn't want to stand up to him either.

Who am I kidding? I wouldn't want to stand up to him even if I did know him. The only reason I ever have is because I know he'd never hurt me. Everyone else, sure—but never, ever me.

I turn away, hoping to shove his order onto Lissa, but she's in the back. *Fuck.*

Since I ran from Dominic's house two weeks ago, I haven't heard a single thing from Alexander—or anyone, except Brooke, demanding if I knew he was responsible for Francis's death.

The note I left behind was clear: leave me the fuck alone.

And for two weeks, everyone did. I moved back in with Rachel and Victoria, got my old job back easily, and I've settled back into my pre-Alexander life.

I wish I could say it's been blissful. I really, really do. But it's been anything but.

When I finally make eye contact with him, my stomach drops. The moment he pushed Tristan into the pool flashes through my mind, and I instantly look away.

"What do you want?" My voice comes out icy and thin.

"I think you already know the answer to that, little bird."

My face heats at the use of my nickname. Who does he think he is, that he can lie to me the way he did and still think I'll fall at his feet whenever he wants?

"Fuck off."

He raises an eyebrow, a hint of frustration showing through his otherwise-cool facade. "When do you get off?"

"None of your goddamn business. I want nothing to do with you."

I feel a presence behind me and turn to find Lissa glaring at Alexander. She's gripping a sleeve of to-go lids so hard we'll have to throw a couple of them away.

"Get out," she says. Her voice wavers, but her chin is held high. "Stop harassing my coworker, or I'll call the police."

Alexander's eyes darken, barely flitting to Lissa for more than a second. "I'm not done with you, Sophia."

"Then you'll have the police to deal with," Lissa says, coming to stand next to me. "Now leave."

With a murderous glance in her direction, he spins on his heels and heads for the exit. Once the door closes behind him, I let myself relax.

"I never should've encouraged you to go out with him," Lissa murmurs, half to herself. She slides an arm around my shoulders.

I'm grateful for the comfort, but I can't take my eyes off the door.

Alexander lied to me. Killed people. Humiliated me in front of all his friends. So why is there a small portion of my heart that's happy that he's still chasing after me?

"Soph!" Lissa snaps her fingers in front of my face. "Get that lying bastard out of your head. He's not worth the brain power."

I told her as much as I could without incriminating Alexander, which wasn't much. But she knows enough to hate his guts.

"I wish it was that easy," I say, taking the sleeve of lids from her. And it's true. I really do wish I hated Alexander. It would make seeing him so much easier.

But no, instead I'm stuck between dread and lust. Betrayal and want. Fear and need.

For the next hour, I do my best to forget about Alexander. But after my fourth messed-up order in a row, Lissa orders me home.

The air is a bit on the chilly side, since it's finally started to cool down. But I decide to walk home anyway. Anything to clear my head.

As I pass by the shop's storefront, I consider taking the long way home. It may be chilly, but the sun is shining, and it's been a while since I've taken a walk just for a walk's sake. In fact, the last time was when Alexander and I hiked through the woods behind his house and I told him the truth about Tristan.

I take a deep breath to keep the tears at bay, ducking my head as a woman walks by. But I only make it a few steps before I run into the human equivalent of a brick wall.

Stumbling backwards, I glare up at him. "Why can't you just leave me alone?"

"What part of *I'm not losing you* do you not understand? I'm not done with you, Sophia. I never will be."

"That's too bad. Because I'm done with you." Even as I say it, I know it's not true—and it shows in the lack of emotion in my voice.

He laughs, but there isn't even a hint of amusement on his face. "Alley. Now."

For a moment, I just stare at him. His dark hair is styled and swept to one side, and his brown eyes pierce mine with such intensity I shiver.

Walking into an alley with a murderer doesn't sound smart, but when it comes to the man in front of me, I rarely am. And while he may have lied to me, I know him—and I know that he'd never hurt me.

So I step a few feet into the alley beside the shop. He follows, hands shoved into his pockets. After a moment of silence, he steps toward me.

"I've missed you, Sophia."

So have I. But I don't say it out loud. Instead, I shake my head. "Is that all you have to say? The last time I saw you, you drowned a man. And all you have to say is *you miss me?*"

I turn to walk away, but Alexander grabs my arm and slams me into the wall. I cringe, expecting my head to hit the bricks, but it hits something softer instead—his hand.

Deadly but gentle.

"Just leave me alone," I whisper, even as my head spins at how close he is to me.

"I don't think that's what you really want. Is it, little bird?" His thumb comes up to trace my jawbone, and I hate how my eyes slip closed at his touch.

"You can't tell me what I feel," I say, but my resolve is weakening—and it's showing. "And you can't tell me what to do."

"I can," he murmurs in my ear, "and I will." One of his arms wraps around me and pulls me into him. "You're going to listen to me, Sophia. Whether you like it or not."

With a grunt, I punch him in the arm, but he doesn't seem hurt at all. Instead, he glares at me for a moment. Then I feel the strings of my apron loosen around my waist before he yanks it over my head.

"W-what are you doing?" I ask, but his only answer is dragging me farther into the alley. "Alexander, what are you—"

He stops me behind a dumpster, shielding us from the view of the street. He grabs my wrists, and I feel the fabric of my apron tightening against my skin. Then he turns me so I'm facing him, keeping me close to the wall.

No, not the wall. The pipes lining it.

"Alexander, don't you dare—" I struggle against him, but he pins me to the wall with his body until he's done. When he moves back, I can only take a step forward before I feel a pull on the apron, expertly holding me to the pipes.

His hand grips my jaw, forcing me to look up at him. "You're going to listen to me, and you're going to do it without struggling. Now, do I need to gag you as well?"

I glare up at him, silent. And not because I'm contemplating screaming. No, my mind is on something he said weeks ago, before I'd given him another chance.

I can read you like a book, remember? And you want me to shove you into the nearest alley and rip your clothes off, tie you up with this little apron, and then fuck you until the whole city hears your screams.

"Do you know," he says with lethal softness, "why I killed my father?" He turns my chin to one side, and then to the other, inspecting me like I'm his next meal.

"No," I whisper, closing my eyes. I can't let him see the want in them. I can't want him. I just *can't*.

"Look at me when I'm speaking to you, little bird." His voice is gentle, but his grip on my chin is anything but.

When I open my eyes, he smirks with satisfaction.

"You didn't think you could hide your arousal from me, did you?" He releases my chin, his fingers ghosting down my neck and stopping at my collarbone.

I stay silent, glaring, waiting. *I just want to go home and cry.* But it's not entirely true. Because he's right—I also want him to follow through on his threat of taking me right here.

His fingers sink an inch or two lower as he says, "For as long as I can remember, my father was an abusive tyrant. Held me to ridiculously high expectations. Tore Brooke down whenever he got the chance, all because he wanted another son. Beat my mother over and over again. Almost killed her a few times."

I shudder as Xander rests his fingers in between my breasts. His voice is so calm, you'd think he's talking about the weather. How can he stay so calm and measured while talking about something so horrible—so *traumatizing?*

"Your mother found out one day. They were at a party, and she walked in on Everly touching up the makeup on one of her bruises. Your parents tried to help her, Soph. Tried to help us. That's why Francis targeted your parents. He needed to strip away every little bit of power and influence from them so he could keep his hold on my mother. On us."

I close my eyes as tears threaten to spill over. How had I never seen it? Is that why Brooke was such a mess during high school? "Why didn't you tell me he was like that?" I whisper. "You promised never to keep anything from me."

"Look at me, Sophia."

I do, biting my lip to hold back a sob.

"It wasn't your burden to carry." His lips brush against my forehead, soft and gentle and . . . caring.

"Xander," I whisper.

He hushes me with a simple kiss. I should hate him for it, but it just leaves me empty and wanting more.

"It took me longer than I wanted to get my shit together. I made up my mind when I was eighteen that I'd end him. When he made me leave you, it was the last nail in his coffin. My only regret is waiting until after I finished college and knew I could handle taking over his companies.

"I thought about you every day, Sophia. And every time I laid my eyes on him, it only made me hate him more. As soon as I could, I forced Brooke to come live with me, and between the two of us we kept mom away from Francis as much as we could."

His forehead drops to meet mine. "He deserved to die, Sophia."

"I'm so sorry, Xan. I had no idea he—" I cut myself off, shivering.

"It's in the past, sweetheart. I need you to focus on the present." He runs his thumb across my bottom lip, and a small moan escapes me. "I need you to understand that I may not be a good person, but I'm yours. I may hurt other people, but I'll never hurt you. And when I do take someone down, I always have a damn good reason."

I dip my head down, staring at his chest. *Tristan.*

"Keep looking at me."

I obey, letting out a breath at the emotions swirling in his eyes.

"He blackmailed you, Soph," he says. I can hear the tension in his voice, and feel it as he presses his body into me. "Scared you. Hurt you. Kissed you." His face darkens at the last part.

I shake my head, holding his gaze, trying to fight the want building up in my chest. "Xander, I just don't know if I can trust myself—"

"No." His tone turns hard, and he grips my waist with one hand while the other wraps around the back of my neck. "I'll ask you again. What part of *I'm not losing you again* do you not fucking understand?"

I can't help it. A small part of me relaxes into him. As my gaze softens, I look at him—really *look* at him—and see the man who's stayed committed to me for years. Who always planned to come back to me. Who wants me, desperately—and will do anything to keep me by his side.

"Think of me as a monster if that's how you have to cope. I don't care. But Francis deserved to die, and so did Tristan. And if anyone—*anyone*-—dares to hurt what's mine again, I'd do the same thing again with no regrets." His voice is hard, but it softens as he says, "That doesn't make you a bad person, little bird."

He tilts my head up, a question floating in his eyes. I only hesitate for a moment before pressing my lips to his. It's everything at once—desperate, possessive, and full of a passion I know I'll never find anywhere else.

I let myself fall into it—into *him*. When his hand slips under my shirt, I arch my back into him.

Maybe it's only been two weeks since he last touched me, but it's felt like an eternity. A hellish one.

He pinches my nipple through my bra, and it sets something off in him. He yanks my shirt up and undoes my bra, but he can't get it off since my wrists are still tied.

"Didn't think that through, did you?" I say in a slightly mocking tone.

With a low growl, he grips it in his hand and yanks. The sound of the fabric tearing echoes through the alley, and I gasp. But I barely have time to react before his tongue swipes over my nipple, sending any rational thought out of my body.

He feasts on me, licking and sucking and pinching and pulling, until I'm ready to scream from the tension. Finally, with a small kiss on my lips, he undoes my pants and shoves a hand into my underwear.

When his finger finds my clit, I cry out. My body has been aching for him for weeks, and now that his hands are finally on me, I'm hyper-sensitive to his touch.

"Remember," he murmurs darkly in my ear. "If you make too much noise, I'll rip this tiny excuse of a pair of panties off of you and shove them into your mouth."

I moan as he rubs my clit, his fingers probably drenched. He watches me, and I don't dare take my eyes off of him again. So instead, I focus on the golden flecks in his perfectly brown eyes.

He wraps his free hand around my throat. The possessive glimmer in his eyes should probably scare me, but instead it pushes me closer to the edge.

When I let out a choked whimper, he shoves three fingers deep inside of me with a groan. And seeing his face, how much he loves pulling orgasm after orgasm out of me, a crystal-clear thought appears in my head:

He's never going to let me go.

Followed very closely by a second one:

I don't want him to. Ever.

The thought does me in, and I fall apart with him knuckles-deep inside of me. His mouth captures my screams as bolts of electricity send my body into a hazy frenzy of pleasure.

When he pulls out, his fingers are glistening with my cum, and he doesn't hesitate to suck it all off his fingers. After he unties me, I reach for his belt, but he catches my wrist with his hands.

"We'll have plenty of time for that later, sweetheart. Let me get you some food before taking you home."

Chapter 19

Alexander

Perfect.

That's the only word I can even think of to describe the woman sitting across from me as she downs her favorite salad, only pausing to take a sip of her blueberry smoothie.

Her bra is in the backseat of my car, since I tore it in half back in the alley. So she's sitting there, her nipples visible through the black of her work T-shirt. And while I'm sure she probably thinks she looks gross, she's anything but to me.

Her blonde hair is pulled up into a messy bun, with strands hanging down to frame her face. But that's not what I care about—no, I care about her lips, soft and pink and slightly swollen from kissing. And her eyes, still slightly foggy from the orgasm I pulled out of her earlier.

My phone rings, and I'm half-tempted to ignore it until I realize it's Blaze's ringtone. With a glare at his face on my screen, I answer.

"What?"

"Hey, is Brooke with you? Have you talked to her at all since this morning?"

My blood runs cold. She may not like being under Blaze's supervision 24/7, but I don't fucking care. She's my kid sister, and I want her safe. "She's not with me."

Blaze lets out a string of curses.

I'm already standing, grabbing a to-go box for Sophia. "Where is she?"

"Fuck, Alex, I'm so sorry."

"*Where is she?*" I hiss, ignoring the concerned look Sophia gives me as I place the to-go box on our table and dump her salad into it.

"I don't know." Blaze lets out a breath, swearing again. "She's just—she's just gone."

I hang up and try Brooke, but it goes straight to voicemail.

Dammit.

"Xan? What's going on?" Sophia is already standing, ready to leave at my command.

Turning to her, I take a deep breath. She places a hand on my arm, and I let her touch calm me. My heartbeat slows slightly, but not enough to dissolve the panic building in my chest.

"Brooke is missing. And I'm not letting you out of my fucking sight."

THE END.

The story continues with Blaze and Brooke in Twisted Redemption.

Bonus Scene

For a bonus steamy scene between Sophia and Alexander, go to subscribepage.io/do-bonus and sign up to my email list.

Author's Note

Thanks so much for reading Deepest Obsession! I had a blast writing it and just letting it be what it is. The series continues with Twisted Redemption and Darkest Retribution.

I've been writing since I was a teenager. Creating different storyworlds and characters was my absolute favorite pastime (okay, okay, coping mechanism). I've always loved romance, especially dark romance with a little suspense sprinkled in, so it's no surprise that it's what I ended up writing.

If you'd like to stay up to date with my latest writings and adventures, you can check out my website elirafirethorn.com or follow me on Instagram, Pinterest, and TikTok @elirafirethorn.

Also By Elira Firethorn

Dark Luxuries Trilogy

Deepest Obsession

Twisted Redemption

Darkest Retribution

Ruthless Desires Series

Blissful Masquerade

Perfect Convergence

Printed in Great Britain
by Amazon

15929035R00144